SUSAN JUBY

Alice MacLeod,
Realist At Last

HarperTrophyCanada™
An imprint of HarperCollinsPublishersLtd

Alice MacLeod, Realist At Last
© 2005 by Susan Juby.
All rights reserved.

Published by HarperTrophyCanada™,
an imprint of HarperCollins Publishers Ltd

HarperTrophyCanada™ is a trademark of HarperCollins Publishers.

First published in trade paperback by HarperTrophyCanada™: 2005
This mass market edition: 2006

HarperCollins Publishers Ltd
2 Bloor Street East, 20th Floor
Toronto, Ontario, Canada
M4W 1A8

www.harpercollins.ca

Library and Archives Canada Cataloguing in Publication

Juby, Susan, 1969-
Alice MacLeod, realist at last / Susan Juby.

ISBN-13: 978-0-00-200828-0
ISBN-10: 0-00-200828-9

I. Title.
PS8569.U324A643 2006   jC813'.6   C2006-902370-0
HC 9 8 7 6 5 4 3 2 1

Printed and bound in the United States
Set in Lynton

For my mother, Wendy, who taught me that the line between being a realist and a romantic is a fine one best walked with laughter.

OF MOOSE AND MEN

A SCREENPLAY BY ALICE MACLEOD

ACT I
SCENE 1:
FADE IN.
WILDERNESS—DAY

A very attractive *GIRL* with an
innovative, asymmetrical hair-
style sits in an ultra-fuel-
efficient four-wheel-drive
vehicle, similar to what an
environmentally conscious star
might drive to the Academy
Awards. The very attractive
GIRL is sitting with very handsome but unconventional-looking
BOY in wilderness setting. They
are talking.

GIRL

I can't believe today is
the day you leave, possibly
forever.

BOY

I know. It's breaking my heart.

*Their eyes begin to sparkle
with tears, which makes them
even more attractive.*

BOY
(With emotion)
I wish this weren't so sudden.

GIRL
*(Understandingly, and
with a lot of soul)*
Life is funny that way.

BOY

You are so understanding! And
soulful! How can I leave you?

GIRL

You must. Your country is counting on you.

BOY

I suppose you're right.

They are interrupted by a noise outside the car. A MOOSE and her CALF walk out of the woods to stand majestically in front of the hybrid sport utility vehicle. As the very attractive GIRL and BOY watch, the MOOSE and her CALF stare at them with a great and terrible gentleness. It's almost as though the wild creatures are blessing them. The MOOSE and CALF fade back into the bush and the GIRL and BOY fall into a passionate embrace.

FADE OUT.

IT'S RAINING HARD KNOCKS:
THE ALICE MACLEOD STORY

Wednesday, June 30

If I hadn't decided to become a screenwriter recently I doubt I could cope with all the things going on in my life right now. But I'm learning that all difficulties are gristle for my artistic mill. I think the first scene is EXCELLENT. It only took about ten minutes to write, so I figure there's a good chance I'll have a first draft of the screenplay done within the week. That will free me up to write *several* screenplays this summer, any one of which may have blockbuster potential.

The great thing about being a screenwriter is that I can use that common technique of spinning straw into gold. So what was a fairly humiliating and dangerous last afternoon with my boyfriend, before he went away for a year with his parents, became in my screenplay a very real and uplifting scene of love and hope.

As I write this, Goose, so-called because of his tendency to look like a goose when he runs (his real name is Daniel Feckworth), is probably on a plane somewhere over the Atlantic. He and his family are going to Scotland for a year while his mother teaches a course at the University of Glasgow. She was called at the last minute after the professor who was supposed to teach the course ate some bad haggis and suffered permanent damage or something. Anyway, the Feckworths decided they'd all go to Scotland for the year. The worst part, at least from my perspective, is that when they get back, Goose will go to university. And not just any university either, but McGill University. In Montreal, Quebec! That's about as far from me, in Smithers, British Columbia, as you can get without leaving Canada.

All that meant our last afternoon together was extremely intense, you know, emotionally. We went out for a drive in my parents' giant station wagon, which my brother, MacGregor, and I call the "Wonderwagon," because it's like the car Wonder Woman would drive if she became an alcoholic stock-car driver. Goose says it's a car with "a lot of potential for the right body man."

I knew Goose would enjoy driving around with me because I got my learner's permit last week, and I'm in that phase where I'm still learning a lot, and driving with me is really exciting. We didn't talk about what we were doing or where we were going, but we knew it was our last afternoon for a long time, possibly forever. We just cruised, laughing and singing along to the Cher marathon playing on the soft favorites radio station.

We headed out of town and up Babine Lake Road, which is very remote and ideal for people looking for privacy. Then I turned onto this little road so we wouldn't get run over by a logging truck, but I must have turned too sharply and then overcorrected because we somehow ended up sliding off the gravel track into a shallow ditch. I put the car in park, turned off the ignition, and listened to the engine tick angrily in front of us.

"We're here," I said.

Goose pretended to radio ground control from the other side of the car.

"This is Slow Rider. I'm here with Learner's Permit. We've got a bogey down. Over and out."

He was totally into his *Top Gun* fantasy, blond hair sticking out in all directions.

The nose of the station wagon had pushed into the dense brush on the other side of the ditch. I looked over at Goose, whose brow furrowed with concentration as he continued his pretend dispatch.

"This is Slow Rider to H.Q. Learner's Permit and I have a situation developing here. Please advise."

He looked over at me, mischievous smile on his face.

Realizing this was the perfect moment, I pulled the condom I've been saving for just such an occasion out of my pocket and placed it quite subtly on the dashboard.

"What do you think?" I asked. "I mean, it's our last chance."

"Oh, Alice," he said, and we fell into each other's embrace. Seriously. It was like something you see in the movies.

Things were just heating up when all of a sudden Goose pulled away.

His hand flew to the dash and he whispered, "Alice–"

A shadow fell over my face as something blocked the light from the driver's side window.

"Don't move."

I couldn't help but turn to see what he was staring at.

Pressed against the window, inches from my head, was a huge, bulbous brown nose. The nostrils flared against the glass, making a huffing noise and leaving a smear of mucus. Then the nose disappeared and a small bovine eye set in a bony head filled the window.

"Oh my god," said Goose, master of stating the obvious. "It's a moose!"

All I could think was that from now on I'd always think of Gooseboy as Mooseboy. I guess I was a bit hysterical. This was followed by the depressing realization that this never happened to young people attempting to lose their virginity in, say, Los Angeles or Toronto.

The moose snorted again and, weirdly, licked its lips, leaving a trail of saliva on the window to go with the snot. Then it disappeared.

"Do you have any idea how dangerous a moose can be?" Goose whispered. "Like if it has cubs or whatever."

"Moose don't have cubs. Bears have cubs," I corrected, and, because I was scared, which always makes me cranky, added, "Didn't you get *National Geographic* growing up?"

"Fine. Fawns then."

"No. Deer have fawns. Moose have, like, calves or something."

"Okay. Calves. Whatever. The point is, this is a dangerous situation. Like in *Cujo*, when that woman got trapped in her car by that dog."

"Check it out," he added. I looked out my window

to see the giant moose standing a few feet away, her head lowered menacingly, the hairs on her hump raised and her ears pinned back. At her side stood a calf, all knobby knees and unlikely angles. The mother moose snorted and bobbed her massive head, as though daring us to try something crazy, like getting out of the car. Her calf began to wander toward us, and the mother huffed another warning.

"I heard moose are disembowelers. They strike with their feet."

"Hooves," I corrected.

"Whatever," he said. "They strike, spill your guts all over your shoes, and then they do the two-step on your lifeless body."

"Give me a break," I said, although now that he mentioned it, I'd heard the same thing.

As the calf bumbled in our direction, the moose charged between us and then pulled up short. The startled calf did a kind of aimless dance and then moved away.

"What," demanded Goose, "is that moose's problem? Start the car. See if we can back up."

"That might make her madder. I don't want her to charge. And I don't want to run over the baby. I've only got my learner's permit."

"What are we supposed to do?" Goose asked.

"Maybe we could—?" I left the thought unfinished but gave a meaningful look in the direction of the condom.

"In a ditched car with a pissed-off moose watching?" he said. "I don't want to sound unmanly or anything, but I don't think I can."

And that was it. Our last chance to consummate our love. Ruined by a moose. We just sat there holding hands until the moose finally left. Then we pushed the car out of the ditch and headed home.

But believe it or not, that isn't the worst of it. On the way there, I told him to go meet other girls.

As if saying good-bye, probably forever, wasn't tragic enough, I decided to make a grand parting gesture. In our last moments together, I said something incredibly stupid. I believe my exact words were, "I'll understand if you want to see other people."

Brilliant. Just brilliant.

"What?" he asked.

"Who knows when we'll see each other again. I don't want to tie you down." Then, swept up in the extreme romance of the moment, I said, "If you love something, set it free." I kid you not. I actually said that.

Again Goose said, "What?" and this time he sounded kind of annoyed.

I felt very noble and womanly. "It's better this way. We should make a clean break. So you have a fresh start."

Goose just shook his head and then we pulled into our driveway to find his parents waiting in their Subaru, looking as well-educated as ever. Moments later, they were gone.

It took about thirty seconds for me to realize that it's fine to make a grand gesture when your boyfriend is just headed across town. He can call and send flowers and reassure you in a multitude of ways. But when he's headed across the Atlantic and basically never coming back, at least not for an entire year, large gestures are probably a bad idea. If he decides to go to university in Montreal, I may never see him again.

The truth is I don't want him to have a clean break or a fresh start. I want him pining over me the whole time he's away. For the rest of his life, if necessary. So why, in our last few moments together, did I essentially tell him it was okay to meet other girls? Because I am a screenwriter. And we like to go for the big finish. Our audience demands it. Maybe part of the curse of being an artist is that you start to do artistic, movielike things in real life.

AN ARTIST EVOLVES:
THE ALICE MACLEOD STORY

Thursday, July 1

As I sit alone here in my room, it's hard to believe that a month ago my life was going well. My family was insane but basically intact, Goose and I were getting along. I'd just finished competing in the Miss Smithers Pageant, which I didn't win exactly, *per se*, but where I made quite a strong showing.

I must have been distracted by the admittedly quite intense competition because it seemed like when I finally looked up, everything around me was falling apart. Goose announced he was leaving. My friend George told me she'd been admitted to vet school in Saskatoon and would be spending the summer at a pre-vet intensive somewhere in Wisconsin. My counselor, Bob, said he was going to a course in Vancouver for the summer. Even Shawn, my martial arts teacher, is away, so the dojo I belong to is not in session. But the biggest blow of all was the realization that my mother has finally managed to get herself in real trouble. In fact, she's been on trial for the past ten days, and today she's being sentenced for crimes she committed during an environmental protest a couple of months ago.

I thought the night she spent in jail after her initial arrest was her punishment, but after the Miss Smithers pageant ended, my parents told me she was still facing charges and could do time. Oh, the embarrassment. My mom and her criminal friends had staged a protest over a developer's plan to build some kind of smelter or plant in a small community called Blueberry that lies just outside of Nanaimo. Unfortunately, the plant, although toxic to the workers and the environment, was going to bring a lot of jobs to the community, so the townsfolk didn't want any interference. When my mom and her activist friends got involved, the situation turned ugly.

Dad said he knew Mom and her comrades didn't have "the support of the people" when he went to spring her from jail and saw a kid working at a gas station wearing a T-shirt that said, PROTEST THIS! and showed a picture of a middle finger. There were people carrying signs outside the jail that read: WE WANT JOBS! and GO HOME HIPPIES! Dad guessed then that Mom might be in more trouble than we suspected.

While my parents have been away at trial, my dad's friend Finn has been staying with us and helping out. MacGregor and I couldn't go because we were in school. Actually, Finn's new boyfriend, Devlin, has done most of the caretaking, including cooking and cleaning, which has been great, because Devlin is a good cook and is nice to talk to. Finn helps out with the TV-watching. To be honest, even though we're concerned about Mom and everything, it's been sort of fun.

Finn and Devlin have only been dating since May but seem to be getting quite serious. Finn is the local used sporting goods salesman and for a long time was the only openly gay man in town. Devlin is the new chiropractor. They make an odd, but to all appearances, happy pair. They're practically living together already.

This is big news because Finn is the king of the short-and-unhealthy relationship. Although he is not attractive or stylish, he's always dating and always getting sick of everybody after a week. With Devlin it's different, and not just because he is healthy in every way that Finn isn't. Finn drinks too much and is cynical and bitchy. Devlin barely drinks and is kind and optimistic. Finn's only exercise consists of getting in and out of his car at various drinking spots. Devlin practices yoga and plays racquetball and does other activities that require coordination and flexibility.

Normally, Devlin is the kind of person (nice and healthy) that Finn tires of. But unlike some of Finn's other nice boyfriends, Devlin isn't a Goody Two-shoes. He laughs at Finn's nasty humor and doesn't pressure him to stop drinking and start working. At least not overtly. Finn may not realize it, but I can see Devlin's influence at work already. Finn doesn't get quite so smashed, and his cutting remarks don't have quite the same edge. As they say in Grade 9, Finn is in *loooove*. As a screenwriter, I can appreciate that. Finn and Devlin are nice together. Seeing them makes me happy. Not that I'd ever tell them that. Plus, I figure screenwriters should have a lot of gay friends. It's just too bad Finn and Devlin are so old. They aren't really friend material.

We knew my parents were due home tonight, and to take our minds off the wait, we decided to play what Finn calls Extreme Games. This involves wearing odd dress-up clothes while playing games for as long as the participants can stay awake. And eating as many snacks as possible.

Finn sat on the couch and surveyed the supplies.

"Mac—go get some chips and that dip in the fridge. Alice, you go get some of those cookies your mother has hidden in the dry goods cupboard—those cookies for old people—digestives or whatever they're called."

I came running back with cookies as Finn sent MacGregor out on another mission. Leaning back on the couch, propped up on the best pillows, he was imperious but benevolent.

"Good job, Mac. You'd better go get us the cards, the Scrabble. And some juice."

Devlin, who was in the kitchen doing the dinner dishes, called into the living room, "Finn, stop ordering them around."

Finn made a dismissive noise. "It's good for them. Builds character."

Finally, Finn decided that we had enough supplies. There was barely any floor visible in the living room under all the snacks and drinks and boxes of games.

"It's going to be a long one, so get comfortable. I'd advise you to layer," he said, and we obliged with gusto.

Because it was summer I wore my bathing suit to celebrate. I had it on under my pajamas, which I'd covered up with a pair of old boxer shorts and one of my mother's winter shawls. MacGregor was slightly more polished in a tracksuit, fly-fishing vest, and a stray fedora. Finn was quite dashing in one of Mom's scarves tied like a cravat around his neck and a large sunbonnet. When Devlin finally joined us he wore MacGregor's toy fire helmet and a pair of flippers.

Finn took the game very seriously. He looked around at us and snorted something about having seen "brothels in Brussels with a more respectable damned clientele." And who knows what he was talking about, but he seemed pleased.

We played a few hands of Crazy Eights to warm up and then cracked open the Monopoly—the ultimate all-nighter game—and settled around it with our fruit punch and chips. It was so much fun that we were almost able to forget that tonight we would find out whether Mom was convicted. We'd only bought a few properties each when I heard the car pull up. I ran to the window, and my heart sank when I saw Dad was alone in Finn's car, which he'd borrowed because ours is not safe on long journeys. He'd obviously taken the ferry from Nanaimo and driven straight through.

I knew the instant I saw him that Mom had been

convicted. What I didn't realize until he came in was just how convicted she was.

MacGregor, Finn, Devlin, and I sat in our dress-up clothes and listened to Dad, who started talking the second he walked in the door.

"It was obvious from the start the case was doomed," he said, in a shaking voice as Finn handed him a glass of juice.

"Kids, I'm sorry I didn't call more often. And I'm sorry I didn't warn you—" he hesitated. "I was just so upset I felt I had to get home. It was just too depressing to talk about."

We all stared sympathetically as he collapsed into a chair. He didn't even seem to register the chaos in the living room.

"The truth is that your mother and the other defendants were too bizarre *not* to convict. They chose this guy called 'Tree' as their spokesperson. Maybe they thought the Raging Grannies hat, which was covered in tinkling bells and silver streamers, would be distracting. Well, I'll tell you what was distracting. Tree's feet. They were these hideous brown misshapen things that ended in long, twisted, rootlike toenails. There are varieties of African monkeys with better-looking feet. Nobody could keep their eyes off them. And this Tree character refused to wear shoes, even in court. Your mother would be home with me right now if Tree'd covered those things up."

We all nodded and shot each other nervous little glances. I wondered if maybe the long trip from Vancouver Island to Smithers had destabilized Dad somehow. Our father is not used to leaving the house. Dad continued, unaware of the growing disbelief in his audience.

"This Tree person would stand out front of the courtroom for the press conferences, speaking eloquently about the developer's shady history, the long-term toxicity of WestPro Tech's operations, and their terrible environmental record, but all eyes ended up on his feet. I can't even begin to guess how much those things must've undermined the message."

MacGregor, with his keen young scientist's mind, speculated that maybe Tree's feet were so bad he wasn't able to wear shoes anymore, or maybe he couldn't afford the special, extra-large, lumpy and twisted shoes such feet would require.

"Chiropractic might have helped," mused Devlin, who as a chiropractor likes to promote his profession whenever possible.

"Or amputation," suggested Finn.

"Regardless," said my dad, "they should have been covered up. It's the feet's fault they're all in jail."

According to Dad, when it was her turn, Mom stood up and made a rambling speech about being a conscientious objector to which the judge replied, "Mrs. MacLeod, we're not trying to draft you. We're trying to determine whether you're guilty of assault, trespassing, and destruction of private property."

When the prosecutor got his chance he asked Mom whether or not it was true that she'd grabbed Pamela Flatt's WELCOME WESTPRO TECH sign and smashed it to the ground and stolen her purse. Mother answered that she was only trying to see if Mrs. Flatt had "children in there."

"She meant pictures of children," Dad explained. "I guess your mother wanted to show Mrs. Flatt that her husband's project would be harmful to children."

Very agitated now, Dad stood up and began to act out everyone's part.

"The prosecutor cut her right off. He said, 'It doesn't matter why you robbed Mrs. Flatt. Did you, or did you not, attack Mr. Flatt's truck?'

"And your mother said, 'I deny that! I was throwing those copies of the company's environmental records at Mr. Flatt, not at his truck.'

"And the prosecutor, who had one of those huge, belligerent lawyer chins, said, 'And somehow in this melee, this fracas, you and several of the other protesters ended up in the back of Mr. Flatt's truck?'

"So your mother says, 'That's right. That's when the fight started.'

"'It didn't occur to you that he might interpret you clambering into his vehicle after you'd snatched his wife's purse as a hostile move and take defensive measures?'

"'There was no need to get violent! We were trying to help Mrs. Flatt see that her husband's project was going to hurt people,' says your mother. Then, like it's relevant, she adds: 'I'm a conscientious objector.'"

My dad fell back onto the couch, exhausted by his theatrics, and reported in a flat voice that our mother had been sentenced to two months in the Vancouver Island Regional Correctional Facility. Nothing even happened to the developer and his wife. They got off scot-free, even though Mr. Flatt gave Marguerite, one of the Raging Grannies, a concussion when he hit her with her own sandwich board.

My mom and her fashion-challenged but well-intentioned friends, including members of the Raging Grannies, Greenpeace, the Sierra Club, and various aboriginal groups, received the stiffest penalties ever handed out for their crime. Their sentences ranged from one month to six months for assault, trespassing, destruction of private property, and resisting arrest.

We knew jail time was an option, but we were still shocked at the length of the sentence. Finn exclaimed in horror, "This is Canada! Murderers only get three months."

"That's what happens when you mess with the capitalist machine," said Dad, obviously reeling at the thought that he was going to be in charge of the family for the entire summer.

Then, finally seeming to register the games and the outfits, Dad said, "So, you guys are playing games."

We nodded.

"Don't let me stop you," he said.

But the game spirit was gone.

As I listened to Dad trying to get Finn and Devlin to stay on with us, I realized it's a good thing I'm a screenwriter now. Other people might waste their time being poets or experimental fiction writers or whatever. But when you're disadvantaged and have a parent in jail, like I do, it's important to be practical. Screenwriting's where the money and prestige are. Our family's survival may be dependent on me selling one of my screenplays for a lot of money.

I figure, between my mother's incarceration and my boyfriend's abandonment, I have enough material for multiple heartbreaking screenplays.

OF MOOSE AND MEN
A SCREENPLAY BY ALICE MACLEOD

ACT I
SCENE 2:
FADE IN.
COURTROOM—DAY

A very attractive GIRL sits holding the hand of a smart and attractive young BOY. You can tell from the look on her face that she's had some hardships in her life, such as her boyfriend moving away. But it hasn't hardened her or in any way made her less attractive. If anything, it's made her face more interesting and thoughtful.

An older *HIPPIE WOMAN stands in front of the JUDGE. She looks a bit irresponsible and is wearing far too much tie-dye.*

JUDGE
(Sternly)

For your crimes and your over-all irresponsibility, I sentence you to ten years in a federal penitentiary.

HIPPIE WOMAN
(Her knees buckling)

Nooooo!

PRISON GUARD begins to lead her out.

HIPPIE WOMAN
(Looks with anguish at her very attractive daughter and smart son.)

I'm so sorry, kids! Please, Annette! Take care of young Antoine. I'm sorry I put my own

ideals before the well-being of
the family. Why didn't I listen
to you? Why? Why?

GIRL
*(With a tremendous amount of
quiet strength, similar to
what she showed when she said
good-bye to her boyfriend in
the car. She has a slight but
very attractive French accent
that you might not have noticed
before now.)*
It's okay, Maman. We will look
after things for you.

HIPPIE WOMAN
And your papa! He will need
care too. He is not strong.

GIRL
*(With a strength and courage
that is wonderful to behold)*
I know, Maman. Everyone needs
me. And I won't let them down.

HIPPIE WOMAN is led out of the courtroom.

BOY
(Looking up at girl)
Is it true, Annette? Will we be all right?

GIRL
*(Kneels to bring her face
level with his.)*
Don't you worry, Antoine.
We will be fine. We are strong.

BOY
(Trust in his eyes)
I know you will help us survive, Annette.

Together they walk from the courtroom.

PRISON GUARD
(Watching them go)
That is one amazing young lady.

So much responsibility for one
so young. And did you know her
boyfriend moved away only days
ago? I don't know when I've
seen such strength.

FADE OUT.

Friday, July 2

Tonight we had a family meeting. MacGregor and
I arrived in the kitchen to find Dad sitting with his
head in his hands. Stacks of bills, presumably placed
there for effect because normally they are hidden in
the odds-and-ends drawer, were spread out on the
table. There were drifts of them. (I expect that it's my
ability to use a word like "drifts" to describe piles of
bills that indicates that I will be an important screenwriter in the near future.)

"God, look at the drifts of bills," I said, so everyone
could enjoy my interior imagery and vocabulary.

"What?" asked Dad.

"Drifts," explained MacGregor. "She said 'drifts.'"

"Oh," said my dad.

"Kids," Dad started. "We need to talk."

Mac and I settled at the table.

"You see, with your mother away"—he said, using his favorite euphemism for her trip to the Big House or the Joint, as it is sometimes known—"things might get a little tight financially."

This was not surprising because my mother made all the money in our family.

"The whole North is depressed," he continued. "So here's the thing, this recession—some might even call it a depression—is taking a toll on our finances. Our candle business is suffering."

I made a snorting noise, and Dad got defensive.

"Candles are discretionary items, Alice. I don't know if you've noticed, but people don't need them for light anymore."

The news that our home-based candle business was in trouble didn't surprise me. The big shock is that it was ever successful with a name like Crystalline Clarity Focus Candles Inc. We—or more accurately, my parents and their assistant—made herb-scented beeswax candles. The candles were very popular for a while, but demand died down recently. My theory is that customers got tired of filling out that ridiculous name on their order forms.

My dad interrupted my thoughts.

"We're each going to have to do what we can. Alice, you and I are going to need to think about getting a job."

"But what about my screenwriting?" I protested. "How will I write when you want me to become a chimney sweep or something? Isn't it a bit Dickens to send the children out to make a living for the family?"

"I'm not sending the children out. I'm sending the teenager out. Besides, you're sixteen. It's not unheard of for people your age to have a job."

"Well, what about you?" I demanded.

"Don't worry. I'm looking too. In fact, I have an interview at Radio Shack on Tuesday afternoon."

That stunned me into silence. My dad hasn't ever had a regular job. Before he met my mom he was a musician. Now he's supposedly a writer, although he hasn't ever published anything. Helping Mom run the candle-making operation hardly counts because he delegated most of the work to our one employee, Betty Lou, who is also my counselor, Bob's, girlfriend, and the bass guitar player in my dad's band—the Hoar Hounds. In spite of how it sounds, "hoar" is actually a reference to a kind of frost that makes everything white. Which is a reference to the fact that all the guys in the band, except my dad, have graying and/or thinning hair. Let's just say they're not exactly Radiohead. The Hoar Hounds get about one gig a year, so it's not like the band keeps my dad on the road eight months out of the year or anything.

If you want to know the truth, my dad, while quite good-looking, is not exactly a go-getter. Things must be desperate if he is thinking about getting a job.

I was just about to say, "Good luck with it," when Mac piped up.

"I can get a paper route," he said.

"Thanks, Mac. But I think this is something your sister and I are going to have to look after. There are laws about child labor. Between the two of us, we should be able to make it through this."

Mac looked unconvinced, and I shared his concern. MacGregor was, to my mind, the most employable of the three of us, even if he is just eleven.

"And if we don't find work?" I asked.

"We have to," he said in a tone that made me start to worry for real.

I'm not resentful or anything, but I can't help but think that other people my age probably spend their summers having fun. They probably go outside a lot (which I admit has never really been my forte), attend barbecues (we're vegetarian and my mom says burnt food is bad for you), and have cool part-time jobs as water-skiing instructors and lifeguards.

Not me. I get ditched by my boyfriend and all of my friends, my mother goes to jail, and to top it all off, I get saddled with my family's financial problems. It's a good thing we screenwriters tend to be strong-minded survivors.

Monday, July 5
Things are looking up! I got my first letter from Goose today. He hasn't met anyone else! He wrote the letter right after he left, so he hadn't had time to be around a lot of other girls, but still.

Some of the letter's too private to discuss. I really like that part. It must have been hard to write with his parents in the car! Goose is very brave. The rest is quite touching and nice too.

I know that we won't see each other for a long time. Maybe you'll move on. Or I will. But nothing could ever change how I feel about you.

We almost shared one of the most important moments of our lives (or at least we tried to) together. That's a permanent bond.

31

I especially hate to be leaving when things are so hard for you, you know, with your mom on trial and everything. But at <u>least</u> she was working for a good cause.

When we get to Scotland we are going on a trek through the highlands and into Ireland so I'm not sure when I'll get access to the Internet. But I will be thinking about you.

Okay, I have to mail this now, because if I wait until we get to Scotland the stamp will cost way more.

Love,
Daniel
P. S. Be on guard for rogue moose.

He is the greatest guy ever. If he didn't live in Prince Rupert, which is at least a five-hour drive from Smithers, I'm sure we would have gotten even more serious about each other and I wouldn't be the last virgin of my generation.

Goose and I met at a fish show in Terrace where both our brothers had fish entered in the competition. I took that as a sign that we were meant to be together. And in fact, we actually sort of *got together,* if you know what I mean, that first day. Unfortunately, my mother interrupted us as we were rounding one of the bases. I'm not sure which one, because I'm not that familiar with the bases. Every time we've gotten together since, which is not that often because he lives in Prince Rupert, something has interfered. Like a moose, for instance.

I wonder what he *meant* by "moving on"?

30 minutes later

I've been thinking about it, and that letter was the big brush-off! The big *sayonara* from Scotland. He is planning to meet other girls. He's making plans to "move on"!

Oh my god! This is almost as traumatic as Buffy's first time, when Angel turns evil right after they do it. Only like I said, Goose and I never actually got to do it. *Per se.*

10 minutes later

Well, fine then. What's good for the Goose is good for . . . well, it's good for me. He's moving on? So am I. I just sent him the following e-mail:

Dear Goose,

Thank you for your letter. Too bad you won't be able to write. I guess you'll be too busy moving on.

Me too. First of all, I'm quite busy socially. Very busy socially. Plus, my screenwriting is really taking off. I'm basically in discussions with some people. Producer-types. You know. They say movie-making is the new novel-writing. I'm pretty much on the vanguard of that whole thing.

Thanks for the memories.
Alice

I'm not sure that quite captures my emotional state. A more accurate reflection of how I feel would have been:

Dear Goose,

AAAAAAAAAAAAAGGGGGGHHHHH HH!!!!!!!!!!!!!!!!!!!!!!!!

.

Alice Heart-Torn-into-Small-Pieces-and-Then-Thrown-Away MacLeod

Oh, Goose, Goose! Why hast thou forsaken me?

Tuesday, July 6
When I got home from the library today, Dad was wearing his best jeans and lying on top of his bed, his guitar resting beside him.

"I'm going to have to sell my guitar," he said in a bleak voice. I was briefly grateful he didn't call it his "ax." He does that frequently, and I find it very embarrassing.

His interview at Radio Shack didn't go well. The manager asked some "out of left field and totally uncalled for" questions about electronics, including asking what DVD meant and made some "outrageous assumptions," including that because of Dad's small business experience as a candle-making kingpin, he could help with payroll. Ha! Mom and MacGregor did all the skilled labor for our business. Dad was more the organizer/delegator. He explained this to the manager, who thanked him for coming in and said he'd be in touch.

Result: We are, if anything, even poorer than when

we started because Dad had to go out and buy a pair of proper shoes for his interview. Even he realized that flip-flops wouldn't be appropriate.

MacGregor joined me in our parents' bedroom doorway to hear the pathetic story of our father's unsuccessful employment efforts. My brother looked worried. I thought about brave Annette in my screenplay, spending all her time looking after Antoine and felt a wave of screenplay-inspired nobility.

"It's okay. Don't worry. I'm going to get a job soon," I announced with a lot of confidence. "I suppose I can write and work at the same time."

I felt like one of those Russian authors forced to compose their masterpieces on toilet paper after being sent to prison for being artistic. Inspired by brave Annette, I wasted no time in getting MacGregor to write my résumé. My employment history's not exactly stellar, so Mac had the idea of making my name and address quite large, so they took up most of the page. Then we left off the dates so no one could tell exactly how long I'd worked at the jobs. So, for instance, when I list July through August at Mountain Lighthouse Brambleberry, the bookstore my mom manages, it could be July of one year and August of the next year or even two years later, which would indicate that I was a very valuable, possibly even irreplaceable, employee. No one needs to know that my own mother fired me a few weeks after I started.

I put down quite a few references: no former bosses for obvious reasons, but plenty of family friends and relatives. My thinking is that potential employers will be so tired from calling all the friends and family they will never get around to asking about work references.

My entire résumé fits on one page. MacGregor, who is a science buff but seems to have a wide range of expertise, says that modern employers are pressed for time, so short résumés are best. I even left off my volunteer activities, such as the 'zine I used to publish and the Miss Smithers competition. Not just because those things weren't unqualified successes, but because I don't have the right ironic detachment about them yet.

All in all, I think the résumé looks good. We printed it on blue paper with a cloud pattern so it's extremely eye-catching.

Wednesday, July 7
I'm not saying I was disappointed when my mother's first letter arrived this morning, but the sight of her

prisoner number and the stamp—CONTENTS CHECKED BY THE VANCOUVER ISLAND REGIONAL CORRECTIONAL FACILITY—didn't exactly make my heart sing the way an airmail envelope from Scotland would have.

I think her plan is to write inspirational letters to each of us once a week. We are probably supposed to treasure them due to how profound they are, sort of like *Chicken Soup from the Incarcerated Parent's Soul.*

ALICE MACLEOD

Box 333 Smithers, BC V0J 2N0

250-847-2333

WORK HISTORY

Mountain Lighthouse Brambleberry Bookstore   *July-August*
Clerk, Salesperson. Specializing in customer service and some security. Shelving new and used books.

Crystalline Clarity Focus Candle Inc.   *May-August*
Candlemaker, Packager. Specializing in pouring candle wax into molds and taking them out. Plus helping with the business end of things. Creative consulting as well. Managed staff of one.

REFERENCES

George Peters, veterinary candidate, Western College of Veterinary Medecine

Daniel Feckworth, currently on sabbatical in Glasgow, Scotland

Karen Field, classmate

Finn Calhoun, owner/operator of Second Sport

Devlin MacDonald, chiropractor

Dear Alice,

Life here is not easy, but it reminds me of how lucky we are to live in a country where prisoners at least get enough to eat. I'm participating in a letter-writing campaign with some people from Amnesty International, and they tell me that the jails in small-town Canada are some of the best in the world.

The other inmates have been very respectful of those of us who are political prisoners. Overall, the atmosphere is very positive. My cellmate, Samantha, who is in here for drug possession (Can you believe this is how we treat sick people in this country? Heaven forbid we should put some money into treatment centers!), said that many in the counter-cultural community supported our actions. They didn't want WestPro Tech bringing their pollution into Blueberry either. Samantha said she would be more than happy to join us for our next action provided she's out of prison by then.

Even though it's hard being away from all of you, I feel tremendous about what we tried to do. The world has reached a crisis point, and I can't live with the idea that I haven't done my best to protect the rights and freedoms of the people and this planet. Each of us can make a difference. Also, I think it's time for your father to take on a few more responsibilities around the house.

I am excited to hear that your screenwriting is going well. The world needs more women film-makers. Women's voices must be heard and women's stories must be told.

Well, darling. Until next time. Stay strong. And remember that a healthy community starts with a healthy family.

All my love,
Diane

P.S. I just got word that Western Living magazine is coming to write a profile about us. It's a piece about environmental activism. Imagine: people who actually do something getting into a glossy magazine! What will they think of next!

Western Living magazine? My mother gets to be in *Western Living* magazine? I'm also very concerned that she is cozying up with drug addicts. I know from what I've read that drugs are rampant in prisons. I can see it now: My mother goes into jail an overly sincere environmental activist and comes out a media star and a Dorito-eating pothead. Or worse!

As if I don't have enough to worry about. Like what Goose might be doing in Scotland.

Thursday, July 8
Today I met my counselor, Bob's, replacement. Her name is Ms. Deitrich, and she's like Bob turned inside out. Bob, whom I secretly refer to as Death Lord Bob, is very sincere and wears all black and speaks in meaningful whispers. He is all about having us—his clients at the Teens in Transition (Not in Trouble) Center—call him by his first name. I doubt Ms. Deitrich even has a first name.

Bob wants us to pursue our dreams. Ms. Deitrich didn't seem remotely interested in my dreams.

Bob gets quite twisted up over me and my problems. He gets involved. He cares.

Ms. Deitrich appeared completely detached. She didn't come out from behind her desk once during our session, not even to say hello. And no matter what I told her, her expression didn't change.

The only thing I learned about Ms. Deitrich's personal life was that before she moved to British Columbia to become a counselor, she worked in engineering in Austria.

Although I'm loyal to Bob, who's been counseling me for a long time now, I kind of like Ms. Deitrich. Things seem quite simple with her. She may or may not care about me, but either way, I appreciate her keeping it to herself.

At our session today, even though I barely know her, I told Ms. Deitrich about Goose leaving and my mother going to jail. It would have taken Bob weeks to get that out of me, but Ms. Deitrich seems to operate from the principle that if I want to talk about something I'll bring it up. And I did want to talk about it.

I told her everything, ending with, ". . . and Goose and I didn't even get to go to any bases because of the moose and before he left I told him it was okay to see other girls and now he's gone and I've ruined everything."

"You are sad because the boy is gone or because he may meet another girl?"

"A little of both, I guess."

"And this 'bases' you speak of. This is sex? You see this as an accomplishment?"

When she put it that way, it didn't sound like much of a goal.

I shrugged. "I guess."

"Loss of the virginity is a milestone. Nothing more. Unless the relationship remains. And this one would not because the boy, he is gone. Yes?"

"Well, yes. But I want him to—" I hesitated. This was Ms. Deitrich I was talking to here, not some caring counselor.

Ms. Deitrich made a tent with her hands.

"Ah, you want to imagine he is your only love and you are his only love forever," she said, only she pronounced it *luff.* "Now we get to it. The great myth of our time."

I didn't know how to respond, so I didn't.

"It is the women who suffer the most from this notion. One true love. Only one. Isn't that what you seek?"

"Well, yes. But—"

"Women look for this one love to make them whole. They wait for love in order to start their lives," she continued.

I didn't know about that. Mostly I didn't want Goose meeting someone else. But she was on a roll so I didn't interrupt.

"You will miss him and you will get over him. He will meet others, and you will meet others."

She sounded so confident of her facts I didn't even

think to argue with her. I just nodded, even though what she was saying was ridiculous. *As if* I would move on. Goose is the *luff* of my life.

"The boys and the bases—these are details made into molehills. And your mother's incarceration. For a good cause, yes?"

I reflected that mastery of the English language didn't seem to be a requirement for counselors. But I refrained from correcting her and just said "I suppose. But my mother's still, you know, *in jail.* And that's not exactly good parenting, right?"

Ms. Deitrich leaned forward in her beautiful suit.

"In this life, we must act on our beliefs. If this means going to jail, that is noble. It is not as though your mother goes to jail for neglect. Abuse. Stealing the cars."

Then Ms. Deitrich got so serious I worried she might strain herself.

"What about you? What are your goals?"

I felt put on the spot and for a moment I blanked. I had no goals other than Goose not meeting anyone else. Then I remembered.

"I'm writing a screenplay. I want to be a screenwriter," I said quickly, grateful that I had something.

"This is very good," she concluded. "So get writing."

And that was it.

After yet another dinner of leftover lentil loaf, the only thing Dad knows how to make, I called my friend George in Wisconsin. I thought she might be sympathetic to my troubles because: a) she recently experienced a breakup (she'd even done it with the boy, so it was doubly traumatic for her), and b) she owes me big-time because I listened to her talk about her breakup for *hours*. But lately every time I call or e-mail her, George and this new friend that she met at pre-vet school are "doing something," and George can't talk or write an e-mail that's more than six words long. It's kind of annoying.

I was just getting started telling her about all my bad news but was interrupted by a lot of giggling in the background.

"Are you listening?" I asked.

"I'm sorry. Liv's just being weird."

Then George herself broke into a fit of giggling. This was very unexpected. George is a humorless laugher and a mirthless chuckler. But she's definitely not a giggler.

I tried again. "So this new counselor told me that Goose and I will get over each other. She obviously doesn't know the depth of our connection. I mean, look at you. You didn't get over . . . um . . . you know, what's his name–"

"Barry. His name was Barry. And to tell you the truth, I—"

"Exactly. You didn't get over him. And you probably never will. It's like that for me and Goose, too."

Our conversation was interrupted by more laughter from the Hilarious New Friend. George never laughed like that when she was hanging out with me. Who knew vet students had so much fun?

"Alice. I've got to go. Send me an e-mail. And say hi to the jailbird for me. That's so cool that she's doing time for what she believes in. I totally respect that."

And then George hung up on me before I even got to tell her about my job search or what's happening in my screenplay. She really hasn't been the same since she went to veterinary school.

7:57 P.M.

I continue to be amazed at how easy screenwriting is. There's practically nothing to it! My third scene is completely from my imagination. There's not a grain of truth in it. And it's still great!

Check this out:

OF MOOSE AND MEN

A SCREENPLAY BY ALICE MACLEOD

ACT I

SCENE 3:

FADE IN.

OFFICE—DAY

*Attractive GIRL, in extremely
interesting and creative
clothes, similar to what a
film industry person would
wear, sits in front of man.*

GIRL

*(Her unusual haircut makes her
particularly interesting to
look at.)*

I'm glad you feel my screenplay
has the potential to break new
cinematic ground, Mr. Tarantino.

MAN

Please, call me Quentin. I was
like you once. Full of dreams

and desires. In counseling for many years. Working at a low-paying video store job.

But I didn't let that stop me. I wrote and wrote, and one day my film *Reservoir Dogs* was made. And the minute people saw that guy's ear come off, they knew they were dealing with real talent.

GIRL
(*Nods. As a fellow artist, she clearly understands exactly what he is getting at.*)
I have no ears, Mr. Tarantino.

MAN
Please, call me Quentin.

GIRL
Okay.

QUENTIN TARANTINO
But you have something other than

49

ears. *Of Moose and Men* has heart.
How does a million five sound?
And a cut of the box office?

GIRL
Whatever you think is fair. I'm
just interested in feeding my
family.

QUENTIN TARANTINO
I hear you, Annette. Say,
what's that accent you have?
It's very sexy.

GIRL
Sorry, Mr. Tarantino. I'm saving
myself.

QUENTIN TARANTINO
I hear you, Annette. And I
respect where you're coming from.

They rise and shake hands.
ANNETTE leaves office.

(*Staring after her,*
with emotion)
That is some woman. She may even
be the next Quentin Tarantino.

FADE OUT.

Friday, July 9

Karen stopped by our house this afternoon and we hung out in my room. She is practically the only friend I have left in town, and she's also the most romantically experienced person know, so I was glad to share my troubles with her.

Karen is a year older than me and is possibly the most popular girl in the history of Smithers. She has taken grooming to a whole new level and somehow manages to combine it with a smoking-and-drinking lifestyle that would make a lesser woman fall into personal disrepair. But not Karen. I've seen her passed out with knife creases in her jeans. It's uncanny. Fortunately for her liver, she's quit drinking since she started dating a guy who works at the local treatment center.

One of the only good things about being a year younger than everyone else in my grade is that I get to graduate with Karen. I got put ahead a year when I went back to school after being homeschooled for ten years. I guess I'm advanced in certain subjects such as English and Social Studies and Coping with Inadequate Adults. Unfortunately, getting put in with older people did nothing for my ability to fit in. It's not like I'm *socially* advanced or anything. The fact that I spend half my time in the regular school and half in the Alternative doesn't help either. I'm lucky that Karen sort of took me under her wing. She seems to find me interesting. She is the head of a clique of popular girls, but they don't dictate who she hangs out with or she wouldn't spend five minutes with me.

"So, fellow grad," she said, "Got your prom gown all picked out?"

With everything going on, I'd pretty much forgotten this was our graduating year. It's not like I've been elected Senior Class President in Charge of Parties.

"I totally forgot."

"What? Being in Grade 12 isn't the most important thing on your mind? What about the parties, the high jinks?"

"Well, between my mom going to jail for the summer and my boyfriend leaving forever, I haven't really had time to think about it."

Karen immediately got serious.

"Yeah, I heard about your mom. That's tough. And Goose is gone too?"

I nodded.

"I'm really sorry. We are going to have to get you out a bit this summer."

"I have to find a job. We're broke." I pointed at my résumé, lying on my desk.

"Well, that should get some attention."

Karen, like my friend George, tends to understate things. I thought again about how odd it is that the most popular girl in town seems to like hanging out with the least popular. Today Karen wore one of her tasteful outfits: a little summer dress, strappy heels, matching purse. I looked down at my old man-style Bermuda shorts and sweater vest and felt painfully frumpy. This summer I'm experimenting with a thrift store look I call "sports fusion." It's intended to show that I am all-around sporty and preppy and not the sort of person who normally has a parent in jail. Sports fusion isn't about track pants and T-shirts, but clothes associated with specific sports. So far I've found a great tennis outfit with a pleated skirt, and most of an antique golfing ensemble including short pants, tam, and the argyle vest. I'm also working on a soccer uniform. I've got the socks and shorts. All I need is the jersey. If I don't get hired on my first film as a screenwriter, there's a strong chance I'll get hired as a wardrobe designer.

But even I had to admit that my modified golf ensemble didn't look that good next to Karen's more traditional, overtly *attractive* outfit. I tuned back in to hear Karen say something about the number four.

"Excuse me?"

"I said, why don't you apply at the Number Four?"

"You mean the *restaurant*?" I couldn't keep the horror out of my voice. "I'm not exactly Number Four material."

"Sure you are. I know someone who works there and I'll bring your résumé in when I go to see her tonight."

I rolled my eyes, but let her take one of my résumés.

"You sure you don't want me to falsify some body measurements to add to that?"

Karen laughed. "It's not that bad."

"Yes it is. I heard Finn say that since Mr. Ho retired, his sons have turned the place into a Hooters with Chinese-Canadian cuisine."

Karen didn't deny the charge. "We'll try to get you an interview with Alvin instead of Trent. Alvin's so stressed out he'll never notice that you aren't exactly Anna Nicole Smith," she said, and then tucked my résumé into her bag.

"What do I know about Chinese food?" I protested.

"About as much as Alvin. He was planning to be a bicycle designer. It was his dad's idea that he help Trent with the family business. Anyway, everything on the menu's numbered. As long as you can count to a hundred, you can do it. Chances are you won't have to go much past four, anyway."

Great. Just what I needed: A little help from my friends.

Monday, July 12
I picked the wrong day to start answering the phone. Normally I let my parents or MacGregor get it. But lately, on the off chance it might be Goose, I find myself racing for the phone like the national lottery corporation is calling to tell me I'm the big winner. Unfortunately, it never is the lottery people or Goose calling. Take the last call for instance.

"Hello?"

"Hi. Is this Alice?"

Damn. It wasn't Goose. And it was too late to put on an accent and pretend the caller had the wrong number.

"This is Alvin. Down at the Number Four. Got your résumé from Karen. Looks good. Are you available for an interview tomorrow?"

My heart started to race. I really didn't want a job. I definitely didn't want a job interview.

"Uh, yeah. Uh-huh. I guess so."

"Yeah. Great. See you at ten thirty."

Then he hung up.

Oh, the horror.

Later

I told my dad about my interview, and he went more or less insane. And not in a good way.

"Great! Fantastic!" he said, sitting up on the couch. "Good work."

He rubbed his eyes and put on his mostly-for-effect reading glasses.

"What can we do to help you get ready?"

I shrugged. "Nothing. I don't know."

"I don't want to scare you, but these interviewers, they'll try to throw you. Ask you questions you don't know how to answer. They try to make it *tough*. To find out what you're made of."

"Oh, well," I said, because really, what else was there to say?

"Just between you and me, you're not the only one with a job interview tomorrow," he continued. "As it happens, it turns out your old man has one too."

"Wow. That's great."

"Yup. And I really feel ready this time. They can throw anything at me and I'm prepared."

My father didn't look very prepared, sitting on the couch in his bathrobe at 5:00 in the afternoon.

"So where's the interview?" I asked.

"Ah! That's my secret. Don't want to jinx it. Anyway, this family's on the right track now. When your mother gets out, we'll be richer than when she went in," he said.

He eased himself off the couch. "Okay, I'm going to make lentil loaf. Where's your brother? Tell him dinner's going to be ready in an hour."

"I think he's at Helen's."

Dad frowned. "Again? What's the big attraction at Helen's?"

Although I didn't say so, Helen's was probably a good place to get away from his hideous lentil loafs.

"Helen's Mac's science partner. Who knows, maybe her family has, I don't know, a good microscope or something."

"That's probably it. But I do think he should be

spending more time at home," he said.

"Yeah, well, I have to go figure out what to wear tomorrow," I said.

Later

I have decided to wear my most businesslike top: a white, secondhand dress shirt with ruffles down the front, probably intended for use under a tuxedo. Unfortunately, the shirt is extremely long and the black skirt I'm wearing with it is extremely short, so my shirttail falls below the hem of my skirt as though it's trying to sneak away. To stop it doing that I have to pull the shirt up at the waist, which creates a bulky yet saggy effect around the middle, as though I recently lost approximately 300 pounds. Because sportswear is so key to my look this summer, I'm going to wear my striped soccer socks with my practical black leather interview-type shoes to indicate that I am only willing to conform so far.

I don't feel ready for the interview. I wish I could be a full-time screenwriter. I wish Goose would come home. I wish a lot of things but it doesn't seem to help.

EMPLOYMENT: JUST ANOTHER WORD
FOR NOTHING LEFT TO LOSE

Tuesday, July 13

As I was getting ready to leave for my interview this morning my dad, who is in no position to judge, said, "My god, you look like the shed skin of a best man."

This from a man wearing a suit that dates back to his brief stint in a Country and Western band; a suit that is shiny and blue and covered in white piping; a suit that looks like it used to belong to Hank Williams.

"Now, I, on the other hand, am dressed for success," he said. "What do you think? I've decided the problem at the Radio Shack audition was that I went too casual."

I nodded but didn't say anything because I am a sensitive person, and my dad really isn't used to being out of the basement for extended periods of time.

He seemed to realize he'd been rude earlier because as I left, he said, "Good luck. And Alice–?"

I turned.

"You'll do great."

"Thanks, Dad," I said. "You too." Even though I had my doubts about both of us.

I walked into the restaurant at 10:30 precisely. The person I assumed must be Alvin Ho was so stressed he might have been in the middle of a bus tour with hundreds of senior citizens clamoring for things in a language he couldn't understand.

"Uh, excuse me," I said, as he shot past the cash register. "Hi, I'm—"

Before I could finish my introduction, Alvin screeched to a halt and leaned in to peer at me. He was a lean, handsome guy with spiky hair. He was dressed as though he was about to start the cycling portion of a triathlon. His right leg was covered in a painful-looking road rash.

"Table for how many?" he asked.

"No, I'm um actually looking for a job. I wanted—"

"Can you come back after lunch?" he asked. "We're really slammed right now."

The elderly man at the lone occupied table got up, tossed down some change, and left.

"But there's . . . I mean, I'm Alice MacLeod. I have an appointment at ten thirty. It's ten thirty," I said. It didn't seem like a good idea to point out that the restaurant was empty.

"Really?" he sounded genuinely surprised. "I guess time got away from me. Well, all right. Have you got another résumé? I can't find the one Karen gave me."

I handed over my sheet of failures and half-truths. I may be a pragmatic realist but my résumé can't afford to be. Alvin looked blinking around the restaurant, and it finally seemed to dawn on him that the place was empty. He ran a hand over his hair.

"Looks like we've got a lull. Let's talk now."

He had me sit at a table and excused himself for a moment. I watched as a bored, robustly built blond girl in a tight black T-shirt and jeans slowly cleared a table. After a few minutes, the girl had almost, but not quite, managed to arrange the cup, spoon, and saucer on the tray to her satisfaction. She fiddled with the items a bit more, then lifted the tray with hypnotic slowness and walked carefully back toward the kitchen, leaving a wet rag sprawled on the table.

Alvin returned, carrying a small handheld tape recorder and a huge binder. He sat opposite me, opened the binder, checked the table of contents, and flipped through to the page he wanted. Craning his head down until his nose nearly touched the page, he read for a moment, then sat up abruptly with a smile on his face.

"Hi," he said, "I'm Alvin Ho. What makes you want to work at the Number Four?"

I struggled to find an answer, but he interrupted me. "Oops, what can I, I mean we, get you? Would you like something to drink? Sorry," he apologized. "My brother, Trent, usually does the interviewing."

"A glass of water would be great."

Alvin called behind him to where the waitress was now wiping a table at the speed of ice forming in a mild winter. "Geena! Can we get a coffee and a glass of water here?"

"Oh sure," Geena replied and continued moving the cloth over the table.

"Super. Thanks."

That interaction seemed to give Alvin new confidence, and he only consulted his binder four or five times during the rest of the interview.

He sat up straighter in his plastic chair, his tight, shiny cycling shirt stretched taut over his chest muscles and biceps. Alvin was practically fit and handsome enough to be in my screenplay. I was still nervous, but found myself warming to him. Or whatever you call it when you start liking someone more than you fear them.

"So what was your name again?"

"Alice. Alice MacLeod."

"Right. So tell me, Alice, why do you want to work at the Number Four? And what attracts you to the hospitality business in general?"

"Um. Karen said I should apply."

Alvin blinked a few more times and snuck another look at his binder for help.

"I see." His fingers fidgeted with the tape recorder and accidentally pressed the play button. A voice crackled out, "So Janice, why do you want to work at the Number Four?" Before I could hear the answer he clicked it off and pushed the machine to the side. Then he noticed we still didn't have our coffee and water.

"Geena, our drinks?"

Geena wasn't even moving anymore. She stood paralyzed, rag poised in midair, mouth open slightly.

"Geena—coffee, water."

Geena closed her mouth. "Oh. Okay."

Alvin smiled again, and bumped his knee on the underside of the table while trying to cross one leg over the other. He let out a soft *ooff.* Then he asked if I had any restaurant experience.

I thought of my trip last spring to Fat Freddy's, an experiment in eating meat that landed me in the emergency room.

"Sure. Yeah."

He looked surprised.

"Really? Wow. Great."

"It's not on my résumé. My experience was, um, quite brief," I said.

Alvin finally managed to get his legs crossed.

"You seem like an ideal candidate to work at the Number Four. At the moment we have enough staff, but we're planning to renovate and change the menu. Go for more sophisticated stuff. Ease up on the chow mein and cheeseburgers. My brother, Trent, thinks we're going to get really busy after that. But for now, maybe you'd be interested in covering shifts on a casual basis? Probably as a bus girl because you can't serve alcoholic drinks. How does that sound?"

"Sure. That's fine."

"What days are you available?"

"Any time really. At least until school starts."

"School's a good idea. Just finished school myself. Brockshaw College. The two-month hospitality diploma. My parents just moved to Palm Springs in their RV, and my dad decided I needed to help my brother out here."

Alvin patted the giant binder at his side.

"Everything you need to know to run a restaurant

in two months. Even if you were actually planning to be a bicycle designer. Amazing! Anyway, tell you what. Stick around, and we'll have you work a training shift today."

Did this mean I had the job? My heart sank at the thought. Alvin was attractive, but not attractive enough that I wanted to work for him.

I cleared my throat. "So does this mean I'm hired?"

"We'll try you out on a temporary basis. We could use someone to help out. Not all the girls have great attendance. We pay minimum wage plus tips. Take fifteen minutes, have a look at the menu, then I'll show you around, and you can work the lunch shift with Geena."

"Do I need to get changed?" I asked, thinking of Geena's tight black clothes, so different from my lumpy interview ensemble.

"Not for your training shift."

I stood up, unsure what to do or where to go while I was waiting.

Alvin handed me a giant menu with a vinyl cover.

"Most of the girls smoke out in the back," said Alvin. "But if you don't smoke, I guess you can just hang out there and read." He pointed to the double set of doors leading to the kitchen.

On my way out the back door of the restaurant I saw the extremely ineffective Geena standing in the bright, noisy kitchen, empty water glass in her hand, blond hair ruffling in the exhaust fan's draft. A thin guy in kitchen whites stood beside her, staring at her as if she was a piece of art he didn't quite get. He caught me looking and smiled as though we both got the joke. I smiled back and thought that maybe filling in at the Number Four wouldn't be so bad.

Later
There are bad afternoons and then there are totally demoralizing car-wreck afternoons that nearly suck the will to live from a person. My so-called training shift at the Number Four was in that last category.

At first, everything went okay. Alvin showed me around and then told me to "job shadow" Geena.

At first, the most tiring part of the training was watching Alvin work. He seemed to get increasingly nervous, and by 11:30 he was jogging back and forth across the restaurant for no reason at all. Then the place started to get busy and everything fell apart.

Geena was patient with me, even though I had trouble making change, running the cash register, carrying plates, and writing up orders.

At first I was worried, but Geena, leaning against the front counter, reassured me.

"Don't worry about it." Even her voice was lazy.

At 11:45 a new customer, standing behind the counter waiting to be noticed, made a clicking noise in his throat.

"Excuse me," Geena admonished him. "We're sort of in the middle of a training session here."

The customer made a huffing noise, causing Alvin, who was seating a table of four women on the other side of the room, to start like a gun-shy dog.

Alvin looked imploringly in our direction, but Geena ignored him. He began to wave his free arm, trying to get her attention, all the while shooting a sickly smile at the customer standing behind us.

"I think Alvin—" I said.

"Don't worry about it. Alvin'll get him," said Geena. "Besides, we're almost on a break."

"But it's starting to get busy." Two more customers lined up behind the foot-stamping huffer.

Alvin was trying to break free of the table of women, each of whom seemed to need a full explanation of every dish: "Excuse me? Excuse me? What is the difference between the Egg Fu Yung and the Almond Guy Ding? What is the difference between the House Special Fried Rice and the regular Fried Rice? Is there MSG in the Sweet-and-Sour Chicken Balls? Why is the sky blue? What makes rivers run downstream?"

After he finally tore himself away, Alvin chugged over, eyes bloodshot, veins standing out on his temple.

"How many?" he asked the first person in line.

"One, for Chrissakes, and make it fast. I've got to be somewhere in half an hour," said the indignant guy.

"Sure, sir. Right this way."

Alvin went to show the man to his table and the other people in the lineup started to shout at him.

"Two! We're two. How long for a table?"

"Hey! What about us? Table for four! What about that table there? Can we just go sit down? We've got to get back to work!"

I started to feel panic setting in, but Geena, in her spaced-out way, was steely in her determination not to work. I tried to hide behind her but the crowd at the door eyeballed me, obviously sensing I was the weakest link.

"You there. Hey." A woman snapped her fingers at me. "Hello—"

I held up a hand, signaling that I didn't understand, hoping they'd think I didn't speak English and would back off.

"It was never like this when the old man ran the place," said a voice.

At that moment Alvin's brother, Trent, swept through the door. He was dressed like a gangster with hoop earrings, heavy gold necklaces, and droopy pants. He pushed his way through the lunch lineup as though he were a VIP at a very cool nightclub. The angry customers stared daggers at him, but he didn't seem to notice, perhaps because his toque was pulled down almost to his nose.

His jeans hung so low that most of his underwear was visible. He wore a mesh shirt through which I could see that his torso was at least as muscular as Alvin's.

"Geena, baby. S'up? S'up?" he said.

Suddenly, Geena came to life.

"Oh hi, Trent!" she squealed. "I bet you didn't know I was working today."

He lowered his sunglasses down his nose and slid a lascivious glance over her. "You're always working for me, baby. And remember, I'm going by T-Dog now, babe."

The vomit factor was off the charts, but Geena didn't seem to mind and gave a tinkling laugh as if he'd just said something incredibly fascinating and funny.

Then Trent/T-Dog saw me.

Something about his flat, blank glance made me want to sneak a look at myself to see if I'd spilled some sweet-and-sour sauce down my front.

Trent sauntered over to the best booth in the restaurant and sat down, like some sort of hip-hop mafia don.

While Geena gossiped with Trent, Alvin and I rushed around the Number Four trying to cope with the lunch crowd. This was complicated by the fact that I had no idea what was going on or what I was supposed to do.

During one lull, I stood, shell-shocked and breathing hard, near the kitchen window.

"You're doing great," said the thin cook, poking his head out of the hole between the kitchen and the dining room. "You just tell me if somebody needs a little something special in their chop suey."

A lot of the customers in the Number Four were older. Okay, make that old. But that didn't make them any less demanding or hungry.

I was only supposed to be running food and cleaning tables, but I kept having to take orders when Geena dis-appeared on one of her breaks. At one table, a pair of senior ladies refused to cooperate.

"What can I get for you?" I asked.

"Same as always," said the smaller lady.

"Ask her," said the bigger one, indicating Geena, who was lounging around on the other side of the restaurant. "Everyone here knows us."

I scurried over to ask what they wanted, but Geena said she had no idea and told me she was going for a smoke.

Back at the table I tried to put a positive spin on things.

"Uh, I'm sort of new. So any information you could give me on what you'd like for lunch would be, you know, appreciated."

"Every day we go through this," sniffed the smaller lady.

"When Charlie Ho was here he always remem-bered our order," accused the bigger one.

"This is no way to make a customer feel special," concluded the little one.

I looked around for help but Alvin avoided my

eyes and when I persisted in staring at him, he disappeared into the kitchen.

Huffing and sighing, the women finally told me what they wanted.

"Number Four Combo. With a cup of decaf."

"Same, but with Chinese tea."

"And no MSG," they proclaimed in tandem.

"I don't think they put MSG on chicken wings," I said doubtfully.

The two women squinted at me from under their visors, and I retreated with their orders.

"Two Number Four combos. No MSG."

The cook grabbed the slip. "Ah. Ms. Martha and Ms. Bernice. Two wings with extra MSG, coming right up."

I hoped he was just joking.

Just before Geena went on her third smoke break, she told me, "Look after Trent. I mean, T-Dog."

I would have rather chopped off my hand and eaten it, but I obeyed. I reluctantly picked up the order pad and walked over to where he slouched in his booth.

By the time I got to him my throat had dried up and all I could manage was a slight, strangled noise.

"Ahghg," I said.

Trent slowly rotated his head in my direction.

I cleared my throat and tried again.

"Can I, um, get you something?"

Trent slid his sunglasses down his nose with his middle finger. He took the sunglasses off, folded them, and put them on the table.

"What do you recommend?" There was no smile in his voice.

I cleared my throat again.

"A sandwich? Maybe a grilled cheese?"

"What number would that be?"

"Excuse me?"

"The grilled cheese. What number is it?"

"I, uh, don't know. I'd have to get a menu. This is just my training shift for bussing tables. I haven't quite memorized the menu yet. I've looked at it, though. All ten pages." I gave a weak laugh. "And I know there's grilled cheese on there somewhere."

Trent softened into condescension.

"What's your name?"

"Alice."

"Well, Alice, we have a few rules here at the Number Four. You shouldn't even be on the floor if you don't know the menu."

Then he flicked his gaze from my waist to my neck.

"And we have a dress code for servers."

I started to protest, "I'm not a server. I'm just—" but was interrupted by a ruckus. It was a customer yelling. At me! Or rather, he was yelling at the plate of food I'd just brought him.

"Sweet Mother of Christ!" a customer yelled. "What the frig is wrong with you people?"

I rushed over to his table.

"I tell you I want a cheeseburger, and you bring me soup? Every friggin' day I come in here and ask for the same thing and every time you screw it up. Is there no competent person left in the whole place? When the old man ran this place I could get a friggin' cheeseburger, NO QUESTIONS ASKED."

Geena, finally back from her seventy-fifth smoke break, sauntered over and in a voice with one of those question marks at the end that made it sound like the matter was up for debate, said, "You can't talk to her like that?"

"High holy hell! I'm the goddamn customer here. Aren't you supposed to at least act like you give a shit if I'm happy?"

Alvin burst out of the kitchen, panic all over his face. His spiky gelled hair was starting to topple, his muscular shoulders were hunched under his shiny yellow racing shirt. He gripped his big restaurant binder as though for support. He rushed to the table to try and salvage the situation as I stood, staring at the bowl of soup. I couldn't even remember if I'd taken the order. I felt like I had heat stroke, like I was about to have a seizure. The room seemed to sway around me. Everyone was yelling. Wanting things. Working in a restaurant was *like being in hell.*

"Sorry sir. Let me just take care of that. She's new," said Alvin, reaching for the soup bowl.

But the enraged customer would not calm down.

"That's what you idiots say every goddamn time. Every single bimbo in here is just being trained. Well, I'll tell you what. Screw this. I've been coming here for fifteen years. Got that? Fifteen years! But I am never coming here again. Never."

The man stood up, knocking over his chair, and stormed out.

Alvin looked over at Trent, who looked over at me, as though I was to blame! A sea of discontented murmurs washed over the restaurant.

"This place has gone to the dogs."

"I don't blame the guy."

"The worst service I have ever seen."

"I'm telling everyone."

Geena was so shaken she had to go and sit with Trent to pour out her troubles, leaving me to wait on her tables while he comforted her.

After the nightmare shift was over, Alvin made me sit at a table in the back of the kitchen to wait until Geena had a chance to show me how to cash out. That's when I heard Alvin and Trent talking in the office behind the kitchen.

"She's not a good fit."

"Oh, come on, Trent. She's all right. She's just supposed to bus and she's catching on pretty fast. That thing with the soup guy wasn't her fault."

"T-Dog," his brother corrected. "There are the *aesthetics* of the thing to consider. We're developing a look here. And she don't have it, brother. We're going to renovate soon. Do the modern Asian club look. Put in some uncomfortable chairs. A bar. Hot waitresses. We discussed this."

"I'm not calling you T-Dog. Anyway, we're getting a bad reputation."

"The crowd will change. We're taking this *uptown,* man."

"People are just supposed to put up with bad service because the girls are hot?"

"Trust me. The hotter the girls, the worse the service. People *expect* it."

"So what do I say to her?"

"Who cares? Just don't call her back."

The back door opened and slammed and their voices went quiet.

I sat alone at the table in a kind of shock. I didn't know what to do with myself.

"Those two are so full of shit."

I looked up to see the thin cook standing at the far end of the kitchen. He looked to be in his twenties and had crooked teeth and crooked brown hair under a white hat.

"So full of shit," he continued, pulling a cigarette out of a red package plastered with health warnings, "it's amazing they can get around without diapers."

I tried to smile, but couldn't get my mouth to cooperate.

"Vincent. Vince," he said, coming forward and extending his cigarette-free hand for me to shake. "Short-order cook and bottle washer. I also hold an advanced degree in asshole detection."

This time I did manage a smile.

"Smoke?" he asked, indicating the package.

"No thanks."

Vince smiled, showing too many teeth in too small a space. The effect was sort of attractive in an old school, un-Hollywood way. He had obviously missed that part of men's fashion school where they taught that men with very curly hair shouldn't try to tame it by putting hats on it, damping it down with gel, *and* combing it behind their ears. Vince had done all three to his and the effect was of hair being severely punished. In spite of all the restraints, odd pieces had broken free of his cook's hat and corkscrewed straight out from his head.

"Okay, well, I better get this smoked before it's time to clean up."

He called behind him, "Hey, Don? You handle things for a minute?"

The other cook, an older Chinese man, nodded, and Vince moved to the doorway.

He looked at me again and repeated, "*Totally* full of shit."

I was still sitting there waiting when he came back in after his break. He hesitated a moment and then said, "This is kind of weird, but would you like to, you know, go out or something? Sometime."

I was startled. He looked a little surprised himself.

But the biggest shock to me was that I said yes.

"Sure. Okay," I said, and my heart started to pound. What was I doing? What about Goose?

"Maybe we could go out for dinner," Vince said. "Saturday? Around seven o'clock?"

I tried to keep myself under control while I gave him my phone number and directions to my house.

And when Geena finally came to help me tally up my tips (which totaled $1.35 in small change) and Alvin told me, with no conviction, that he'd "be in touch" and handed me my wages for five hours of work, I barely heard a word.

But when I was leaving and the nice cook said, "So I'll see you Saturday," I nodded and gave a quick, awkward wave. Once I got outside I started to run.

Wednesday, July 14

I arrived home yesterday afternoon, my head reeling at the thought that I had betrayed Goose, to find my dad lying on the couch.

I took one look at him and turned back to ask MacGregor, who was in the kitchen making herbal tea, what was wrong.

"The interview was at the feed store, and it didn't go too well," my brother informed me.

"Please tell me 'feed store' is just the new name you're using for the grocery store."

"No. Like feed store for animals. Hay and oats. Salt licks."

"But dad can barely tell a cow from a horse. How is he going to work in a feed store?"

"He's not."

I followed my brother back into the living room, where all the blinds were pulled and my dad, still wearing his drugstore cowboy suit, lay with one arm hanging over the side of the couch onto the floor. He looked like he'd been shot.

"Here, Dad." Mac put the cup of tea on the coffee table beside him.

"It was the suit," muttered our father. "Why did I wear this suit to an interview at a feed store?"

I silently agreed that it was probably not a wise choice. But I kept quiet. The man was obviously torn up.

"I should have worn overalls. Your mother has a pair. They're yellow, but . . ."

We sat quietly in the chairs across from him.

"I just . . . " began Dad before his voice trailed off again. "It seemed like . . . I mean, after all, wouldn't the damn farmers know what feed they needed?"

We nodded.

"That guy in there. He didn't need to make it so plain he thought I was a poor excuse for a man when I didn't know the difference between lambing feed and calving pellets. I mean, how *material* is that anyway?"

He continued in the flat monotone. "Now I know exactly how men felt in the Great Depression. Robbed of pride. Their ability to care for their families stolen from them."

MacGregor and I exchanged glances. This was all just a little over the top coming from a man who'd never held a real job.

"I checked into getting a paper route," said MacGregor. "It turns out there's only one person who delivers papers in Smithers. And he's also the Community Events reporter."

"Good man, Mac," said my father hoarsely. "I appreciate that you tried." Then he opened one eye and looked at me, standing there in my wrinkled, ill-fitting interview outfit. "How did your interview go? Where have you been anyway?"

"Uh, it was okay. They actually had me work a shift."

Dad opened both eyes and turned his head.

"So you got the job?"

"Not exactly."

He and Mac both looked at me.

I debated whether to tell them the truth and then decided against it. No decent father or brother would want to know their daughter/sister is considered too ugly to employ.

"I'm sort of on-call, I guess. So I probably won't work too much."

"Good for you," said Dad. "Get a foot in the door. That's the way to do it." His eyelids dropped shut again. "A person's just got to get a foot in the door."

With that, I retreated to my room to figure out what to do about the fact that I was about to cheat on my boyfriend who'd only been gone for TWO WEEKS! What kind of person would do that? Even if Goose did say that stuff about moving on.

I should really cancel my date with Vince. It was made under duress: I'd just discovered that some people consider me too unattractive to be seen in public. I still love Goose, but all it took was another guy asking me out and I said yes. How psychotic is that? Am I so insecure that I'm willing to go out with any attractive, nice, charming guy who asks? Does that make me a slut? How can I be a slut when I'm still a virgin? I am very confused.

I've been thinking about the whole attractiveness thing. I know I am not traditionally pretty, you know, *per se*. I mean, I've got innovative hair and experimental clothes and my face is, well, my mom says it's distinctive. She means it as a compliment, but that's not the kind of thing you want to hear from your own mother. On the negative side, she calls a lot of her weirdest, most patchouli-smelling friends distinctive. On the plus side, she once called Parker Posey the same thing, so I choose to take heart from that.

I always sort of thought that one day I'd blossom into this pretty person. But the experience at the Number Four suggests that people who are into traditional good looks are never going to find me attractive. Don't get me wrong. I don't care. Even to consider it is shallow. Goose thinks I'm fine the way I am. And so does Vince, apparently. Not that it matters what boys think.

There's only one answer for this. Writing! A new scene in my screenplay will help me think.

OF MOOSE AND MEN

A SCREENPLAY BY ALICE MACLEOD

ACT I
SCENE 4:
FADE IN.
RESTAURANT—DAY

A GIRL wearing an attractive short black skirt and beautifully ironed white dress shirt stands in an elegant restaurant. She is being interviewed by an attractive MAN who, under his Armani suit, is obviously quite fit.

                    MAN
So, you'd like a job at Chez Chic?

                    GIRL
    *(Her accent may be more than
     just French. It may also be
     a bit Spanish. This gives her*

a certain *Jennifer Lopez–*
courageous striver sound.)
Yes, sir. I would.

MAN
Aren't you that girl who
recently got the film deal
with Quentin Tarantino?
Where did all your money go?

GIRL
(*Bravely*)
I cannot say.

Another man bursts into the
restaurant. He looks a bit like
Jamie Oliver from The Naked
Chef, *only thinner. He is very*
attractive and has celebrity
quality.

OTHER MAN
(*Breathlessly*)
Wait.

MAN and GIRL turn to stare.

                    OTHER MAN
I can't let you do this!

                    MAN
What? What has she done?

                    OTHER MAN
She has given all her money
to her family. Except for the
money she gave to me so I could
start my celebrity chef chari-
table foundation to benefit
hungry orphans.

                    MAN
Wow. And to think I thought she
looked weird.

                    OTHER MAN
You couldn't be more wrong and
shortsighted.
*(Speaks to the GIRL, who stands
humbly and attractively to the*

*side. He has an excellent light
lisp, similar to Jamie Oliver.)*

Please come be a producer on my
new reality TV show in which
I feed and train young hungry
orphans!

GIRL
*(Who in the dim light of the
restaurant looks a bit like
Michelle Pfeiffer and also
like Jennifer Lopez. Sort of
a combination of the two.
Delicate yet feisty. Tender yet
resilient.)*
I don't know what to do. I have
to support my family. And be a
writer. And not be dependent on
men.

OTHER MAN
You wouldn't be dependent on
me. I'd be dependent on you.

MAN

But what about me? I've just
realized that you are the
key to the success of this
restaurant.

GIRL

Please. I must think. I have a
true love. Who has moved away,
but still.

Men begin to fight. As they are
fighting, GIRL slips out of the
room like a delicate yet resil-
ient ghost.

FADE OUT.

I feel much better. Maybe I won't cancel my date
with Vince just yet.

Later

My mother's letter today was almost inspirational,
even if it was a bit too long. Say what you will about
my mother, she cares what happens to her family,

even if we aren't her first priority or anything. In my last letter I told her that Goose had gone and I may have mentioned that I was going to give up on boys, at least until Goose comes back.

Dear Alice,

This will probably embarrass you but I just want you to remember that you are an amazing young woman. I know you will miss Goose. He is a very special person, and you were great together. But life has many twists and turns. All I ask is that you stay true to yourself.

As a talented person, you have many things to concentrate on. Just don't be surprised if you're not as "off boys" as you thought. They have a way of showing up when you least expect it. At least, they did when I was a teenager.

Now my cellmate, Samantha, is someone who might want to take some time off boys! Her boyfriend came to visit yesterday, and I could feel his negative energy from across the waiting room. No wonder she was on crack. Five minutes in that kind of energy and I'd take

*up drugs too! It's too bad because before he
came to visit she was doing so much better.
Now she is fretful and irritable again.*

*·Promise me that you will never spend time
with a lover who doesn't respect you. Your
father and I have had our troubles, but at the
heart of our relationship is a deep friendship
and bedrock of respect. Many of the women
here have never been treated with dignity. I've
asked your father to send me my copies of*
The Beauty Myth *and* The Second Sex. *I'm
going to begin consciousness-raising sessions
for all the women with self-esteem problems.
I suspect we're going to need a big room!*

*Remember darling, saving the world starts
with saving each other.*

*All my love,
Your mother*

She is too much. I know she means well, but how
unrealistic can you get? Saving the world. What will
she think of next!

I have this sneaking suspicion she's planning to use
our correspondence to create some kind of *Tuesdays*

with Diane–type book. I mean, she's not dying or anything, but she's trying a little too hard to be timeless. She has never called me "darling" before. Not once. Using the word "lover" with your sixteen-year-old daughter is just plain *wrong*. Besides, who signs a letter "Your mother"? Oh well, her feminism sessions should be interesting. Just think: empowered women with criminal know-how.

Thursday, July 15

Betty Lou came over today so my dad could officially lay her off from the candle business and tell her the band is on hiatus. I'm sure neither of these things came as a surprise. She hasn't worked for weeks and the band hasn't practiced or had a gig since their one and only appearance at the Sweetheart Ball.

Everybody but me loves Betty Lou. I figure she appeals to my counselor, Bob, her boyfriend, because she's a dyed-black person too—hair, clothes, etc. But she takes it a few steps further, and is thoroughly ventilated with piercings and covered in tattoos. Once, I asked her if she worried about her tattoos sagging as she got older, and she pointed at her shirt, which read: I HOPE I DIE BEFORE I GET OLD.

Can you imagine? This is the person my mental-health professional is dating!

Before she came over, Dad was saying how sad he was about the layoff. He thought Betty Lou was the best assistant candlemaker he'd ever met.

When he saw that I wasn't too torn up about it, he accused me of not understanding her. "She's a genuine rebel, Alice. I thought you'd appreciate that."

I pointed at my tennis outfit. "I'm quite conservative and preppy now, Dad. Duh. Where've you been?"

"Under that exterior she's a very sweet girl," he continued.

"Under that exterior is a body crying out for help—iodine, bandages, you name it."

"Well, even you have to admit she was a godsend for the band."

That part was true. Before Betty Lou joined the Hoar Hounds they were the least energetic band in existence. Every song was a slow song. And they spent pretty much all their time talking about the old days, when they were supposedly very popular with a certain type of person, who I figure must've had more than a nodding acquaintance with sedatives. But when Betty Lou joined they sped right up. And she did bring the group a much-needed *edge*, what with all her piercings and tattoos.

My mother also knew I wasn't crazy about Betty Lou. She once said, "Don't be afraid of her just because she's a strong woman who refuses to buy into commercial notions about how women should look." Then she added, "Besides, jealousy doesn't become you."

"Jealousy! Ha!" I exploded, right on cue.

It's not that I feel jealous of Betty Lou. Once, when she was working, pouring wax into the candle molds, and I was sitting in the basement complaining to her about my life, she looked at me and said point-blank, "Kid, you have no idea how lucky you are." That was it. She didn't yell or anything.

She said it like she was almost bored by me and my problems. Betty Lou *shamed* me. So now I don't like her.

I could never talk to Bob about my feelings because he dates Betty Lou and is always going on about how *real* she is. As though I'm not! I can't see how a few tattoos make Betty Lou more real than me. This is part of the reason I'm going conservative now. (It may also be a reaction to having a parent in jail.)

In spite of my feelings about her, when she came

into the kitchen today, I said hello. I may not like her, but I am afraid of her.

"What are you up to this summer?" she asked. As if she cared.

"We're all trying to get jobs," my dad informed her. "Alice even had a shift at the Number Four."

Betty Lou's eyebrow piercings rose.

"It didn't work out. I'm not Number Four material," I informed her.

Betty Lou laughed. "Good for you." Then she said, "I'm opening up a yarn store. I could use some help getting set up."

Apparently, her grandmother died and left her some money, and she is going to go into business for herself.

"A yarn store?" I couldn't keep the doubt out of my voice.

"Don't knock it till you've tried it," she said, reminding me why I don't like her. But she had me. I couldn't turn down a job in front of my dad.

"Sure. That'd be great."

"Excellent. Come down to the store Monday afternoon. Maybe I'll teach you to knit. That is, if you're not too cool."

She was making fun of me! It's not that I'm too

cool to knit: It's that my image can't afford it. I'm already alone on the fringes. Just imagine how popular I'd be with a pair of needles stuck through my bun as I sat, surrounded by knitted acrylic washcloths. Betty Lou has so many tattoos she can get away with doing a grandmotherly activity like knitting. I can't afford the loss of edge. Even if I am a cool screenwriter.

For a town that's supposed to be depressed, Smithers sure does seem to have a lot of jobs for its youth.

YOUR CHEATING HEART

Friday, July 16

In a miracle of bad timing, I finally got an e-mail from Goose.

If he'd just written a bit more often I wouldn't have accepted an invitation to go on a date tomorrow night with someone else. Sure, he was hiking through the Highlands and Ireland and all that. But I'm sure there are Internet cafés in the UK.

Also, I couldn't help but notice that his message didn't exactly pull on the heartstrings.

Hi Alice,

Scotland is okay so far, but the food is not great. Everything is deep-fried and comes with mayonnaise. If you order a salad, you get a heaping cup of mayo with one piece of iceberg lettuce poking out. I'm concerned that I may develop scurvy from lack of vegetables.

The trek was okay. Lots of fields and heather,

and many, many sheep. We're in Glasgow now.
It's so gray here that it gets dark at about 2:30
in the afternoon. My parents don't want me to
go out after dark because Glasgow is filled with
bald guys in black boots who are "not to be
messed with." I'm a grown man of 18 so I'm not
going to tell you about that. I've met a couple
of nice people. One is from Sweden. Her family
just moved here, and her dad will be teaching at
the same university as my mom. Her English is
very good.

I would call you, but it's about 12 pounds a
minute. I hope things are good for you.

Love,
Daniel

Her? Sweden? As if I care about how good her English is! Is Goose moving on with some Swedish girl? And what's with the food report? It seems to me that if he's been eating fried food, an Internet café couldn't have been far away!

I have no idea what any of this means. What am I going to do about my date with Vince? If I go, am I cheating? And if I am, does that mean Goose is allowed to cheat? Maybe he already has with some Swedish girl who probably speaks better English than I do and looks like a supermodel. I know all about the Nordic races and how they are unnaturally tall and good-looking. Hmph. What can I say to him? I've got to think this over carefully.

Later
Here's what I came up with:

> *Dear Daniel,*
>
> *How nice to finally hear from you. I've been very busy. I have quite a few new friends too. One is a chef from Spain. At least originally. His English is excellent, and he's quite tall and coordinated. He's good at everything.*
>
> *All the best,*
> *Alice*

Okay, so I'm not sure if Vince is Spanish. He has dark hair and an olive complexion. He *could* be Spanish. It's possible.

That clinches it. I'm going ahead with my date.

I'm torn between working on my screenwriting and choosing an outfit for my date tomorrow. I rented *Say Anything* last night. Because I am a screenwriter, I feel like it's basically my duty to watch quite a few films.

Later

My favorite scene in *Say Anything* is when the very hot John Cusack stands outside Ione Skye's bedroom window with a boom box held over his head playing "In Your Eyes" by Peter Gabriel. My second favorite scene is where they are in the back of his car and he gets all shaky due to the intensity of their physical interaction. I watched the scene about eight times, and I'm almost certain they are doing it. Or they just did it. One or the other. I bet it would have been like that for Goose and me if we'd actually gone all the way. Although it's just as well Goose didn't get all shaky like Lloyd did, because the moose might have misinterpreted it as a hostile gesture and charged the car.

I wonder if Goose is about to have a just-friends date with the Swedish giantess supermodel who speaks good English. Not that it matters.

Still haven't decided what to wear.

Saturday, July 17
8:03 A.M.

I woke up to another e-mail from Goose. Apparently, he was offended by my last e-mail.

Alice,
Spanish? Coordinated?
Please.
Daniel

I haven't written back. I'm starting to understand why long-distance relationships don't work.

8:17 A.M.
I probably misunderstood Vince. He doesn't really want to go out with me. He was just being nice to the plain and possibly even unattractive girl. Since that was the case, I have decided against wearing sportswear on our date tonight. Instead I will wear an aspiring-filmmaker outfit of jeans and a plain T-shirt. And a trucker hat, which is practically *de rigger* for everyone in the film industry. It is my most neutral outfit, designed to indicate that I don't care about appearances and, as far as romance goes, my expectations are low. I figured that if Goose saw me

he'd realize I wasn't doing anything wrong. Not in an outfit like that. And not that I care what he thinks, as indicated by the e-mail I just sent.

Hi Daniel,

I'm not sure what you mean by "please." You're not the only one who can get new friends from different countries. I may be stuck in Smithers, but sometimes the mountain comes to Mohammed.

Anyway, let's not bicker over e-mail. I hope you are having fun. With the giant Swedish girl who is just a friend? Or maybe more? To be honest, I don't really want to know.

In fact, I don't think we should e-mail for a while. It kind of bums me out.

I'm going to send this before I write something I regret.

Alice

At first it seemed like kind of a mature e-mail. So why am I so depressed? I am not in the mood for a date.

Vince will be here in just over ten hours.

10:45 A.M.

I watched *Say Anything* again. I am quite a bit like Ione Skye's character. She is gifted and kind and a bit of a lone wolf. The big question is: Who is the John Cusack figure in my life; the loyal and brave romantic who is undeterred by rejection? Is it Goose? Or Vince? Just under eight hours until I find out.

11:15 A.M.

Dad just asked me, not very nicely, to please stop pacing between the living room and the kitchen. He is reading *What Color Is Your Parachute?* for the millionth time. I don't know why he bothers.

12:02 P.M.

Maybe I should e-mail Goose and apologize? Then I should cancel the date. The stress is killing me.

2:30 P.M.

Dad and MacGregor just watched *Say Anything* with me. They both cried a bit in the sad part. You've got to give my mother credit: She's obviously had a profound influence on the men of this family. They are both quite sensitive and in touch with their emotions.

So is John Cusack's character, even though he's a kick-boxer. I miss martial arts. Not so much that I ever practice, though. Shawn, my sensei, is going to kill me when he gets back.

I wonder if Vince thinks about me as much and as selflessly as John thought about Ione.

2:55 P.M.

Hey! Maybe I should pretend this date is a martial arts test! That way I can be all detached about it.

I told Mac my plan but he didn't get it.

"You're going to attack the guy?" he asked.

I suppose it was a logical question.

"No. I'm going to be sort of, you know, clinical. Treat the date like a martial arts test. Or an experiment."

"Don't you get sort of nervous before your martial arts tests? Remember how you kept saying you were going to throw up the last time?"

"Well, that test was special because it was part of the Miss Smithers Pageant Talent Competition. If I ever take a regular test, I'll be much calmer."

Dad, who was eavesdropping instead of focusing on the career guidance in *What Color Is Your Parachute?*, said, "It seems a little cold to treat a date like a test."

"I'm not going to *tell him* it's a test."

"People pick up on these things. Why don't you just approach it like he's a new friend you're getting to know? Not someone you have to beat up to pass a test."

Doesn't anyone in this family have any loyalty to Goose?

"It's always nerve-racking to meet new people," said my dad. "God, I remember the first few times I went out with your mother."

"I thought she asked you out and talked the whole time."

"That's true. But it was still tense."

I looked at my dad with new respect. That was the best conversation we'd had in months!

3:05 P.M.

Apparently, the strain of being involved in our lives was too much for Dad. He just went for a nap. MacGregor's gone to Helen's. Again. I like having him home. I'm going to have to come up with some plan to get him to stick around a bit more often.

Only three and a half hours to go until my date.

6:15 P.M.

Oh my god! How could I have fallen asleep! He'll be here in 45 minutes and I don't even have on my low-expectations/I'm-not-really-cheating outfit!

9:30 P.M.

I couldn't believe it when the bell rang right at 7:00. I rushed to the front door, still pulling my T-shirt down, to find Vince, in his own low-expectations outfit of a flannel shirt over a T-shirt and jeans. Although something about the cologne and wet hair curling around his collar suggested that maybe his expectations weren't *that* low.

"Hi," I greeted him.

"Hi."

We stood mute for a minute.

"Are you ready?" he asked.

"Oh, right."

I turned to get my sweater, and we went outside. I felt sort of grateful that my dad was still napping and MacGregor was out. Why did I feel so guilty? Goose was gone. This was just-friends.

The door opened behind us. Damn. Spoke too soon.

My dad stood in the doorway in his bathrobe, rubbing his eyes.

"Hey," he said blearily. "Have a good time." Then he stood there, waiting for an introduction.

"Uh, Dad, this is Vince."

Vince gave a tight smile and shook my father's hand. I could see the questions starting to churn in my father's eyes, so I got us out of there.

"Okay, see you." I said and practically pushed Vince out the door.

"What time will you be home?" my dad called after us.

"I'll have her home by—" Vince began, but I interrupted.

"Home by nine. Not going far! Bye!" I gave Dad a pointed wave.

Reluctantly, my father stepped back in the house.

In the driveway I looked around, trying to spot Vince's car.

"Did you park on the street?"

"No, I, uh, didn't actually drive."

I didn't know what to say about that. I'm not the type to be won over by a nice set of wheels and leather interior or anything, but it's the rare guy in Smithers who doesn't drive. Walking is actually considered bad manners here, unless you are wearing a backpack and headed up a mountain.

Vince shifted the jean jacket he was carrying and coughed into his hand.

"I thought we could, you know, walk."

"Sure."

We trudged out of our driveway and down the street in silence. When we reached the corner, he spoke again. "I do know how to drive."

I nodded and tried to be encouraging. "That's great."

That made him laugh.

"I'm just not allowed to drive for a while."

"Oh." Pause. "Why not?"

He snuck a look over at me and grimaced quickly, as though in anticipation of tasting something bitter.

"Well, I sort of got an impaired charge. You know, for drunk driving. I've made a few lifestyle changes, and I get my license back in three months. But right now, I'm driving my shoes."

"Oh."

"Still want to go for dinner?" he asked.

I shook my head to clear it. He misinterpreted the gesture and stopped dead.

Rushing to clear up the confusion, I blurted, "No, I mean, yes. Sure. I still want to go for dinner. I was just thinking about what you said."

"I know. It's kind of messed up. It was a stupid thing to do."

I nodded as though I knew exactly what it was like to get an impaired driving charge. Like every second person I knew had one.

For some reason it felt like we'd crossed some line where now everything we would say to each other would be very heavy and deep. In fact, I started trying to come up with some profound inner secrets or at least a shameful and, ideally, criminal past incident to share with him and quickly realized that: a) I wasn't deep or profound, and b) my life wasn't exactly filled with dramatic lawbreaking events. It was middle class (minus the money). It was tragedy- and crime-free, at least so far (my mother and her activism excepted).

As we walked I kept sneaking looks at Vince. He was that kind of thin that looks strong and flexible. No extras. No gym muscles. Only the bare essentials. His crooked teeth gave his face a slight edge, like he was either very funny or very poor. The thought that he was disadvantaged financially, maybe even more than us, started to make me feel bad for him. As I walked with him I started to feel touched by hard times too. It was as though Vince's drunk-driving confession put him behind a glass wall of tragedy. Yeah, that was it. Vince lived behind a glass wall of tragedy. And only I could reach him.

"I got beaten up," I found myself telling him. "A couple of times."

Vince kept walking, but turned his head to look at me.

I felt compelled to continue.

"I don't, uh, I don't fit in all that well. With others." Then I started to list every hardship I could think of.

"I got drunk a while ago. And my mom's in jail. For protesting stuff," I added, breathless.

Vince stopped, fit a cigarette in his mouth and lit it, still watching me in a slightly bemused but not unfriendly way. He exhaled a stream of smoke toward his chest and gave a half smile, tilting his head toward me.

"Thank you, Alice."

The rest of the date, if that's what it was, was nice. We walked along the access road to the biggest hotel in Smithers and went into the café rather than the dining room.

"You like the Lodge?" he asked.

I shrugged, not wanting to admit that I'd never been before. That I'd never really been anywhere. Except that one time I took MacGregor to Fat Freddy's to eat meat.

We slid into a booth and I realized that I *was* on a date, even if it was a just-friends date. And I was on it with someone who is practically a man. I began to wish I'd worn something a bit nicer than my screen-writing outfit of plain jeans, T-shirt, and sweater. I took my trucker hat off.

We sat quietly until the waitress came to take our drinks order.

While we were sitting there it occurred to me that if Vince was poor, I should offer to pay half. I wasn't sure I had enough money on me. What if he ate a lot of expensive items like shrimp melts and steak sandwiches? Those things were $12 each! What if he drank? I definitely didn't have enough money for him to get drunk.

When the waitress showed up I asked for water, just to be on the safe side.

"You sure? You don't want a pop or something? This is on me, you know," he said.

"Are you sure?"

"Do you have a job?"

"No. Not really."

"So it's on me. Hey, I'm just glad you agreed to go out with me," he said, looking right into my eyes and making me go all squirmy with embarrassment.

Then, because I am so suave, I blurted, "How old are you?"

"Twenty-two."

"Oh," I said.

Another silence.

"Does that bother you?"

I shook my head again.

"And you?" he asked.

"Almost seventeen," I said, because five months goes by quickly.

He blinked quickly and looked down for a second.

I kept sneaking glances at him. He was so close to me. Just across the table. His skin was dark, the planes of his face angular. His eyelashes were long, like a girl's.

"So–" we said again, together, then laughed awkwardly.

"You said something about a boyfriend. . . ."

"He moved away to go to Scotland for a year. And then he's probably going to school. In Montreal."

Vince nodded. "I guess you'll be going away to school, too."

"Maybe after next year."

"Yeah, you look like the type."

"What does that mean?"

"Smart. Nice. Like your family is, I don't know, educated."

I laughed. "Not very. Are you going to school? Or did you?"

"Cooking classes. At the college. First one in my family to go past high school."

Soon I was telling him about how all my friends had left or were leaving.

"You'll leave too," he said.

"Maybe not. You didn't."

His smile was sharp, the crooked teeth glinted in his face.

"Exactly."

After dinner, he asked if I wanted to go for a walk around the Perimeter Trail.

The trail encircles the whole town. Walking it is popular with middle-aged ladies. Sometimes my mom and MacGregor and I walk around it. But I'd never really seen any other young people, especially a young guy like Vince, on there. He and I caught the path where it passed behind the hotel and followed it to where the train tracks lay in the shadow of Hudson Bay Mountain along Railway Avenue.

We talked. We talked about the Number Four and we talked about me and we talked about him. And he was funny and he listened and he made me laugh. As we walked through the little playground in the park near the high school, I said something that made him laugh and he grabbed my hand, squeezed it, and let it go. It might just have been a friendly gesture, but when he touched my hand it practically burned.

If that date was a test, Vince passed it.

Sunday, July 18
Okay, so I'm obsessed. Completely obsessed.

Here are just a few things I no longer care about:

1) being abandoned by my boyfriend;
2) being abandoned by my friends;
3) my mother's incarceration;
4) poverty, the prospect of nuclear war, and environmental degradation.

It comes as a relief. It's like Vince has moved into my head and rented every single inch of available space. Let's face it: There was quite a bit of unused room up there.

But my father, who is not aware that I am obsessed, insisted on trying to intrude on my thoughts.

"So." He hesitated. "How was your date?"

"Fine."

"Your friend, what was his name again?"

"Vince."

"Right. He seems nice."

"Yup."

"He's, uh, he'd be a little bit older?"

"I dunno."

"Damnit Alice, stop farting around. How old is he?"

"Nineteen," I lied.

Dad sighed.

"I don't know. That's—"

"Only a year older than Goose. And I thought I was just supposed to enjoy the date. Get to know him."

"Where did you meet him?"

"At the Number Four. Where he *works*," I said, turning the knife. "Anyway, is the interrogation over?"

"It's not an interrogation. Did you tell your mother about him?"

"He's just a friend. God," I said and made a move to escape.

"Wait, I forgot to mention. Finn and Devlin came by today—"

"Stop the presses. There's a rare event."

"For your information, since he met Devlin, Finn comes over far less often than he used to. Anyway, the point is that Finn told me that the Bulkley Valley Junior Backpackers need a part-time guide/counselor. I gave him one of your résumés to pass along."

I was thinking about Vince so I didn't bother answering.

"Hello? Alice? Did you hear me? You might get a call about a job from someone with the Bulkley Valley Junior Backpackers Club."

"Sure, whatever," I said.

Later
Amazingly, even Goose's last e-mail barely penetrated my obsession.

Hi Alice,

Maybe you're right and we shouldn't talk for a while. Just remember, I'll be here if you need me.

Daniel

I didn't even write back. What is there to say?

I wish Vince would call.

Monday, July 19

I have to work for Betty Lou today, and even though I'm dreading it, I'm grateful too. It will give me a break from wondering why Vince hasn't called.

I've channeled some of my anxiety into my art, but I still have quite a bit left over.

OF MOOSE AND MEN

A SCREENPLAY BY ALICE MACLEOD

ACT I
SCENE 5:
FADE IN.
CHEZ CHIC—DAY

The handsome, restaurant-owning
MAN and the Jamie Oliver-looking
OTHER MAN are still fighting
and the very attractive GIRL

stands looking at them, shaking
her head wryly.

GIRL
Please, stop it, both of you.
Stop fighting over me as an
employee and love object.

The MAN and OTHER MAN immedi-
ately stop fighting. They turn
to her, awaiting her next words
with baited (bated?) breath.

GIRL
(Speaking to the OTHER MAN with
terrible sadness in her voice)
You shouldn't have made me wait
for your call.

OTHER MAN
But Annette! It's what I had to
do. It's what all men do.

GIRL

(Her accent, which sounds like a cross between J.Lo's and some French person's, becomes more pronounced because she is very upset.)

Well, now I have to do what I have to do. Find a job on my own. Be independent from men seeking my favors.

The GIRL sweeps out of the restaurant. The MAN and the OTHER MAN watch her go, dismay in their eyes and also on their faces.

MAN

What have we done? I should have hired her right away and seen that she wasn't weird. She is actually amazingly special.

OTHER MAN

I should have called her right

away. She's too good to wait
around for a phone call.

They both look after her, naked
yearning on their faces. But
she is gone. Off to find a job
in which she can excel on her
own terms and not be dependent
on men.

FADE OUT.

Later

Betty Lou's new store was tucked away in a nothing little plaza off Main Street. An old laundromat
sat on one side and the Eternal Anchor tattoo shop
on the other. At the end of the complex was the
MuscleMart, which has been closed ever since the
guy who ran it got busted for selling steroids.

I peered in the windows of the store. All I could
see were empty shelves. The door was slightly ajar
so I went in.

"Hello?"

No answer. I tried again. "Hello?"

Maybe Betty Lou went out without locking up. I

walked farther into the store. There was white dust on everything and the room smelled of newly sawed wood and glue. A stack of cardboard boxes lined up against the wall caught my eye. One was partly open. After a quick look to make sure I was alone, I walked over and looked into the box. It was stuffed full of clear plastic bags filled with yarn that looked like incredibly long, flexible feathers in brilliant colors: ruby red, cobalt blue, and canary yellow.

I reached a hand into on of the bags. The yarn was so soft I had a sudden urge to dive right into the box. I picked up one of the balls of yarn and, after admiring it for a moment, rubbed it on my cheek the way kids do with the satin edging on blankets. Looking at all the yarn in that one box and imagining all the yarn in the other boxes made me feel like a rich person in a room full of money: satisfied and acquisitive all at the same time. Who knew yarn was so great?

"Nice, eh?"

I was too embarrassed even to jump. Instead I jammed the yarn back in the box and turned around.

"Uh, yeah. It's nice."

"That's the first shipment. I don't even have anywhere to put it all yet. There are about fifty more shipments to come."

Betty Lou looked as radical as ever but somehow more relaxed. Happy. She was in overalls and a tank top, and her tattoo-covered arms had smears of white paint on them. She rubbed her hands on her legs and moved behind the counter.

"You ever knit before?" she asked. When I shook my head no, she said, "You're going to like it," and then she threw me a ball of the yarn I'd been fondling. "All the cool girls do."

Helping Betty Lou wasn't so bad, really. I cleaned the floors and started writing labels to put on the shelves. She promised to show me how to knit next time. We also talked more than we ever have before.

"So where's that boyfriend of yours?"

"Gone. Scotland."

"Bummer," she said. And I felt like she really understood.

"I miss him. But I just met this other guy. He's older. It's kind of confusing."

Betty Lou ran a forearm and wrist over her head. "That's exactly what it is. For all of us."

"I kind of like the new one. I saw him Saturday

and it was really great and everything. But he hasn't called."

"Maybe he's on the three-day plan."

I looked at her.

"Guys don't call for at least three days. It's supposed to show that they're busy but they haven't forgotten you. It's like this rule they have."

Her words sent a shot of hope through me.

My experience at Betty Lou's yarn store suggests that knitting is going to be the perfect complement to my career as a screenwriter. I'm not just going to be any old knitter either, but more of an *art* knitter. My stuff'll be so creative it'll sell for thousands. Goose may be hanging out with Nordic supermodels and wearing kilts (without underwear, according to what I've heard), but I'm going to be a one-woman creativity factory!

Later

When the phone rang tonight I jumped on it. Maybe Vince was on the two-day plan!

"Hello!" I tried not to sound as breathlessly eager as I felt.

"Hello," came the voice, deep, male.

My heart started ricocheting around in my chest.

Vince! Vince!

"You sure sound in a good mood," came the voice.

"Heh-heh," I replied, smooth as always.

"Are you available tomorrow?"

Should I play hard to get? Flirt? What to do? What to do?

I chose Option Number Two.

"Definitely available for you," I said, only I stumbled over the word "available" and then rushed through the rest of the sentence to try and make up for it.

"Well, thanks," came the voice, "especially if you just said what I think you did."

"Heh-heh," I said, cementing my reputation as a silver-tongued vixen.

"You're the first person I've interviewed. With luck you'll be the only one. Finn says good things about you. And your résumé was pretty cool."

My heart dropped back into its usual place with a thud.

"Résumé?"

"The one with the clouds. A good choice for someone who wants to work outdoors."

"Yeah, well."

"My name's Evan. I know it's not a lot of notice, but I'd like to interview you tomorrow at seven in the second parking lot up the Ski Hill. You know where that is, right?"

"Seven?" I asked, a little wildly. "As in A.M.?"

"Yeah, I thought we'd do it before the kids arrive for their hike. That's okay, right?"

I cleared my throat. "Sure, yeah. That's great."

"Excellent. See you tomorrow then," he said and hung up.

Great. Just great. Now I knew why the youth unemployment rate was so high: I was getting all the jobs. I wanted to call Goose and tell him the bad news about how I seem to be the most employable person in all of Smithers, but then I remembered his last e-mail. We aren't talking. And Vince isn't calling.

In desperation, I tried calling George. It was two hours later in Wisconsin, so I hoped she wasn't sleeping.

She picked up on about the fortieth ring.

"Hey! Are you up?" I asked.

George's voice sounded a bit fuzzy. "Not really."

I heard a voice in the background.

"What are you guys doing?" I asked, suddenly jealous that George had a new friend and I had no one.

George cleared her throat. "Nothing."

Giggling in the background. Weird noise in the receiver.

"Sounds like you're having fun. I'm glad one of us is."

Then she totally cut me off again!

"Alice, I'm sorry. We're just, um . . . I have to go. Look, we'll talk later, okay?"

"Sure," I said, trying to keep the bitterness out of my voice. Here I was spending all our family's non-existent money to call her long distance, and she couldn't even be bothered to have a conversation. The only time a person is allowed to be that self-centered is when she's in love!

In the end, the only person I could think to tell my troubles to was my inmate mother, so I wrote her a long letter. It's odd, but I actually sort of missed her. I know I missed having Mac around. I've started to wonder if he's moved to Helen's.

Then, I had an idea. I should give him a birthday party. Maybe that was how we could lure him back into the fold. The concept was genius! I was just sorry I had the interview tomorrow or I would have started planning the party right then.

THESE BOOTS WEREN'T MADE FOR WALKIN'

Tuesday, July 20

I learned two things at my interview for becoming a counselor/guide for the Bulkley Valley Junior Backpackers Club.

1. One interview outfit does not work for all jobs.
2. Luck plays an important role in any job-getting process.

I showed up at the interview site, which was the parking lot nearest the ski lodge on Hudson Bay Mountain. Because it was a job interview, I wore my Interview Outfit including a pair of big, black competence-illustrating shoes. I nearly died when I saw who was going to be interviewing me. I'd seen him around town a few times and noticed him because he was so blindingly good-looking that he made me feel like putting on sunglasses. He's probably in his early twenties, but when a person's that good-looking, age is difficult to tell.

"Hi there, I'm Evan," he said, sticking out his hand for me to shake.

"Alice. I'm Alice MacLeod. I'm here about the job." And then my mouth took off on me. "I've seen you before. I mean, I saw you. On the street. You're old . . . er. Older, I mean," I finished lamely.

He smiled hugely. "I'm sorry I don't remember you. I'm leading the Backpackers this summer." He frowned slightly as he took in my outfit. This made him look extremely smart as well as handsome. "Well . . . I had planned to do the interview and then have you join us for a hike to see how you connect with the kids. But your shoes are—" Words failed him as he gazed at my practical shoes.

I could feel my open and positive facial expression, the one I use for job interviews, begin to fall.

"I can hike," I said.

Blond God looked doubtful.

"I left my hiking stuff at home because, I, uh, wanted to prove a point."

He seemed to expect me to finish the story so I searched my brain frantically for the rest of it.

"With the shoes. That it's good to be prepared. Equipped. Like that. But, um, sometimes you have to, you know, adapt. Just in case you're not prepared."

He smiled and I focused on his dimples for courage.

"Because you never know when you're going to have to hike unexpectedly. Like if your car breaks down and you have to walk. In, like, non-hiking clothes. For instance."

I took a huge breath. It may even have been a gasp. Damn. Another job down the tubes.

But he said, "That's an interesting idea, Alice."

Yeeessss! I thought, but just said, "Thanks."

"Let's sit over here and talk a bit about your background and why you'd like to work with us," he suggested.

I followed him to the picnic bench and sat down.

"So tell me a bit about yourself." He was doing the smart, serious frowning thing again, making it hard for me to concentrate.

I'm going to be seventeen soon. I've been in counseling for about ten years and my hobbies are getting beaten up, losing jobs, and finishing almost nothing that I start. Oh yeah, I want to be a screenwriter, but my mom's in jail, so I really need what artistic people call a straight job.

"I've always loved the outdoors. And um, kids. I really, you know, like working with people. And kids."

"Why do you think you'd be a good guide/counselor for the Bulkley Valley Junior Backpackers Club?"

I wouldn't.

"Due to, you know, liking kids. And the outdoors. Et cetera."

"Can you tell me a bit about your previous work and volunteer experience as it relates to this job?"

I was fired from a New Age/secondhand bookstore for gassing the chemically sensitive owner with Buddhist Temple–blend incense. The job was originally gained through nepotism (my mother was the manager).

More recently I was fired or at least not hired at Number Four Chinese/Canadian Restaurant after my first training shift due to lack of good looks.

I'm an active member of Teens in Transition (Not in Trouble) Counseling Club. Awarded Longest-Attending Member with Outstanding Major Issues That Show No Signs of Easing Prize.

Rod & Gun Club candidate in the Miss Smithers Pageant. Lost.

Member of Asskickers Dojo. Our sensei is away and I haven't practiced once since he left.

"I have worked in retail and am involved in a martial arts club where I work with Bees. I mean, young people."

"Nothing outdoors?"

No. Thank god.

"I help my father in our, uh, organic garden. We are active hikers. I'm extremely interested in, um, Nordic skiing."

"Really."

"You bet," I said.

"You are the first person I've interviewed for the job. In fact, I hadn't even advertised it yet when we got your résumé from Finn. I thought you could come out with us today for a short hike. See how it goes. It would be cool if I didn't have to talk to anyone else."

Evan smiled gorgeously at me, and I did my best to return the smile before asking, trying to disguise the fear in my voice, "Hike? For how long?"

"Just a short one. Maybe two and a half hours there and back. For an average hiker. Some of our kids can make it in one and a half."

"Terrific," I said.

"You're sure you can hike in those shoes?"

"Absolutely. Are you kidding? They're great."

My shoes were great all right. Each one weighed about eight pounds and the exaggerated rubber treads had an annoying habit of trapping rocks and sticks and other sizable debris. These were strictly

Job Interview Shoes. By the time I got up a mountain I'd have half the trail stuck to the bottom of them. I'd look like an Ent on the march to war.

As we finished the interview, the Junior Backpackers started to arrive, dropped off by parents in minivans, station wagons, and Ford Fiestas. Soon, small- and medium-sized outdoorsy folk swarmed everywhere, outfitted in tan and khaki and accessorized with brilliantly colored hats and backpacks.

I stood beside Evan, who alternated between greeting the kids and their parents and explaining the club.

"Our kids are between ten and fourteen," explained Evan. "We've got thirty enrolled for the summer session. We also run the club in the winter. Then we do skate-skiing and classic skiing. Avalanche awareness. Sounds like that might be right up your alley."

Another wan smile from me.

"Hey, Wallace. Where's Renée?" Evan called out to a boy in a long black coat who stood motionless in the parking lot, his back to us.

Rather than answering, the black-clad boy, who appeared to be around fourteen or so, turned, letting his head fall dramatically toward his shoulder, leaving his mouth slack, and pointed at the ground, the picture of exhaustion. His face was stark white and his eyes were rimmed in black. I saw that crouched behind him was a plump girl of about the same age. She wore a brilliant red-and-orange kerchief over an exploding mass of hair, as if Anne of Green Gables had gone for a spiral perm rather than a dye job.

The girl stared into her open backpack.

"Hey Renée," called Evan.

"Hi," she said, without looking up from the depths of her backpack. "I'm just looking for my lunch."

Evan waved and the bleak boy gave a deathly little wave in return.

"A few of the kids are here," continued Evan, "to work on self-esteem, discipline, or personal achievement."

"So it's like boot camp?" I asked, suddenly interested. "You mean they come here instead of going to jail? I've read about stuff like that." I was thinking that if this was like a prisoner/guard relationship it might be more bearable. I'd get to be in charge and lord my authority over people. In that kind of situation my heavy black shoes would make perfect sense.

"No. More like an athletic day camp," corrected Evan.

I tried to hide my disappointment. "Oh."

Then Evan introduced me to Jeanine, the other counselor, a robust, ruddy-cheeked girl with an Australian accent.

"That's quite the outfit," she said.

"That's quite the accent," I replied.

She laughed. "Right then."

After counting the kids, Evan introduced me. "Everyone, this is Alice. She'll be joining us today. If you have any questions during the hike, or need help or advice of any kind, just ask her. I know she'd be more than happy to help. And of course, there's always Jeanine."

The Junior Backpackers rushed to join Jeanine and Evan. They probably wanted to ask detailed questions about the Latin names of flora and fauna we passed as well as Evan and Jeanine's philosophies regarding the meaning of life. And possibly they wanted to ask about Evan's beauty regime, which was obviously very successful.

As we started the hike, I very naturally fell into last position, which, if you think about it, is the anchor position, suitable only for the very responsible. In seconds I had enough rocks and sticks trapped in the treads of my shoes to landscape a small garden. Convicts dragging balls and chains made less noise and had better freedom of movement.

Fortunately, there were three Junior Backpackers who were just as slow. I stopped to dislodge some boulders from my shoes and asked one of them for the time.

"Eight oh three," announced a Junior Backpacker, who looked about eleven years old.

"No problem then," I said. "The hike's just two hours. We've been going for at least a half hour already."

"Three minutes," said the kid, after consulting a large instrument that hung around his neck. "Three minutes and 22.7 seconds, actually."

"Uh," I said.

"You have no idea what you're doing, do you?" said Wallace, the goth boy, who spoke as though he was so bone-tired he could hardly open his mouth. He sounded much older than he looked.

"Oh, Wallace," said Renée, who'd finally pulled her head out of her backpack and was now trudging unhappily uphill with us, red-faced from the effort.

"I'll have you know I'm extremely outdoorsy," I said, trying but failing to keep the snotty, non-counselor-approved tone from my voice.

"Then why are you dressed like a waitress in a failing Italian restaurant?" asked Wallace.

"How old are you anyway?" I asked, impressed that he knew what a waitress in a failing Italian restaurant would wear. I wouldn't have had a clue.

"I'm fourteen."

"Going on forty-five," wheezed Renée. "Don't mind Wallace. He's a member of the Bulkley Valley Junior Curmudgeons Club."

"Ohhh, curmudgeon!" cooed Wallace. "Somebody's retaking English this summer."

Renée rolled her eyes, and I stopped to take a small sapling from my left shoe.

Later

After an hour even the three kids, who were incredibly slow walkers, were starting to complain about my pace.

"Could you hurry up?" urged Instrument Boy. "I've got piano practice tonight."

"It's fine. I'm just taking note of the scenery. You know, the trees and grass and stuff. For future reference. In case *you guys* have any questions."

My attempts to make them feel guilty didn't work.

"It's okay," consoled Renée. "The first hike is always the hardest. I don't mind going a bit slower."

"You should have worn different shoes," lectured Instrument Boy. "You have to be prepared for anything when you go into the back country. Proper gear is essential."

"Like Ted here, for instance, is practically prepared to open his own outdoors store," huffed Renée, who it turns out had been sentenced to the Junior Backpackers by her parents, who were concerned about her weight.

"Ted here's prepared to be a giant pain in the ass," grouched Wallace, who revealed that he was sent by his father, a logger who was having trouble with the fact that "his boy" wore eye makeup.

Ted would have kept pace with the born-to-hike types ahead of us, but he was smaller and younger than most of them and completely overloaded with gear. Besides the global positioning system, which hung around his neck in a special purse, sensibly labeled "Ted's GPS," he had a large knife strapped around his chest, an avalanche beacon, infrared goggles strapped to his knapsack, and a giant canister of bear spray in a holster attached to his belt. In addition, he wore three sets of bear bells, which made him sound like a lost goat herd.

"I'm thinking Ted might be just a little afraid of the great outdoors," Wallace said.

"Oh, shut up, Wallace," said Ted and Renée, together.

"All of you be quiet!" I said, then realizing that might sound a bit harsh, added, "Please."

"So, Ted," I said. "Do you know my brother? MacGregor MacLeod? He's your age."

"What school does he go to?" he asked.

"Muheim Elementary."

Ted shook his head. "No. I go to St. Joe's."

"Oh," I said. So much for my attempt at personal conversation. But Ted had more to add.

"You know, if you'd go faster, we wouldn't argue so much. Jeanine always makes us go so fast we can't talk."

"This one can't go any faster, dummy," Wallace pointed out, which was rude but basically accurate.

"Don't worry. This is the first and last hike you'll ever have to do with me."

"Why exactly were you trying to get a job as a hiking guide, anyway?" Renée wanted to know.

"I need the work."

"Why? Don't you have any money?"

"No. My family is very poor. My mother's in jail."

"Really!" said Wallace in a thrilled voice.

"It's true. So I have to help out."

"Can we ask you another question?" said Wallace.

"Okay."

"Why is your hair like that?"

"What do you mean?"

"I mean your hair is pretty out there. I like it, but it is sort of unusual."

"I only get it cut by this one guy in Prince George. And we only go to Prince George about once a year. So I cut it myself. It's supposed to be a bit shorter than this. Also, I'm a screenwriter, so hair isn't that important to me," I lied.

"It's very messed up."

"Hmph," I said.

"No. I mean it as a compliment. You're quite weird," he said thoughtfully.

I ignored him.

"Seriously. You are practically the only person I've ever met who makes me feel normal, and I've only known you for an hour. I think having you around will be good for my self-esteem."

"Well, I'm sorry I can't help you out because I'm not going to be around," I informed him. "I don't like hiking and I'm not good at it."

"You were a total freak in school, right?" he said, as though I hadn't spoken.

"I'm still in school. But for your information, I was homeschooled for ten years. Now that I'm back, hardly anyone notices me, weird or not."

"So you could show us how to survive what is basically a cruel and inhumane system?"

"That's a little melodramatic, isn't it?" I asked.

"No," he said fiercely. "It's not. Not all of us have the option of being homeschooled. Regular school may be hell, but hanging out with Harold and Maude, twenty-four seven, would be the end of me."

Renée explained, "His parents aren't really called Harold and Maude. That's just the name of this movie he likes. It's about a younger man and an older woman. Wallace's mom's six months older than his dad."

"Eight months," Wallace corrected. "If you stay on as a counselor we promise not to make you go too fast. Come on. Do we have a deal? I mean, you need the money, right? Because you're all poverty-stricken and everything."

"I'm sorry, but I'd rather starve."

After the hike I said good-bye and good luck to the kids. I felt a bit sad. It's always hard to say good-bye to fellow oddballs. I sat on a concrete barrier, every muscle aching, fatigue leaching my last traces of energy.

Evan came over to where I was slumped.

"Well, I don't know what you said or did to those kids but you made quite an impression. I've never seen them so enthusiastic about anyone. To be honest, they're pretty miserable most of the time. Especially Wallace."

I tried not to show I knew what Evan meant, and kept my gaze on the ground.

"Anyway, they are totally set on you joining us. So how about it? Are you interested? This isn't a full-time gig or anything. We just go out once or twice a week. But it's a blast. I think you'll like it."

I noticed Wallace and Renée standing across the parking lot staring at me, and then I looked up at Evan, who was training every ounce of his good-lookingness at me.

And I found myself nodding, almost in spite of myself.

"Right on!" said Evan. "Having someone who can deal with those two is going to be worth their weight in gold."

I tried to smile.

"And you have such a righteous phone manner," he said and grinned.

What have I gotten myself into?

Later

Vince called. Betty Lou was right: He's on the three-day plan!

I'm so relieved because I know we made a connection. People are supposed to call after something like that. I told him about my job interview.

"This guy named Evan runs the club. He seems pretty nice."

"I guess he'd be one of those Tarzan of the Great Outdoors types."

I laughed. "Yeah. I suppose. He seems pretty fit."

I could hear Vince puff on his cigarette.

"Hmmm," he said, then, quietly, as though speaking to himself, "danger, danger."

"Pardon?"

"Nothing. I would have called earlier, you know. But a person's supposed to wait."

I felt a smile break over my face and the blood rush to my skin.

"My next day off is Saturday," he continued.

"Okay."

"I'll pick you up at six thirty."

"For dinner?"

"No. Six thirty in the morning."

"Are you serious?"

"Totally. It's not just outdoorsy types who get up early, you know."

"Well, I don't really—okay."

"Don't worry. You'll have fun," he said fiercely before he hung up.

I don't understand why I miss Goose but have no trouble liking Vince.

OF MOOSE AND MEN

A *SCREENPLAY BY ALICE MACLEOD*

ACT II
SCENE 1:
FADE IN.
MOUNTAINTOP—DAY

Exceedingly attractive, out-doorsy-looking GIRL strides along high mountain pass. Her thick blond hair is in long braids and she is wearing state-of-the-art outdoorswear. She looks incredibly fit. Camera closes in on her face. We see that it's ANNETTE! She has obviously been hiking for quite a while, because her hair is very long now. She looks as though the fresh air has given her new confidence. She is basically at one with the mountain. She is followed by THREE YOUNG PEOPLE, who clearly

respect and admire not just her
looks and filmmaking ability,
but also her extensive wilderness knowledge.

YOUNG PERSON #1
Annette! Annette! How did
you move beyond the confusion of lost love and career
disappointments?

*YOUNG PERSONS #2 and #3 lean
close to hear the answer.*

GIRL
*(With a lot of humility, and
not the false, irritating kind
either, but rather the kind
that comes from being deep and
thoughtful and spending a lot
of time in the wilderness and
being quite spiritual)*
Well, children, I had to leave
the world behind and take to
the mountains. Because that's

where I found my inner truth.
My personal clarity. Plus
spirituality.

YOUNG PERSON #2
But Annette! What about the
restaurant business? What about
show business and being the
next Quentin Tarantino? How
could you leave it all behind?

GIRL
It's like this. I had to be
strong. And keep moving. In the
open air. When life gets too
hard, go to the mountains.

YOUNG PERSON #3
(With awe in his young voice)
That's incredible advice. And
when I'm older I plan to measure every woman against you,
Annette. And not just because
you have long blond braids and
are very attractive, but also

because you care about young
people and the wilderness and
understand romance.

*The THREE YOUNG PEOPLE all nod
in agreement. Then they pick up
the pace so they don't get left
behind as the girl strides over
a hillock and disappears behind
a dale.*

FADE OUT.

Karen stopped by this afternoon. After I told her
about all my news (and there was a lot!) she read the
first few scenes of the screenplay. I could tell she was
impressed. She laughed in several places, which was
odd, given that it's not really funny, but I think it was
laughter of admiration. You know how sometimes
when you're reading something, and it's just so good
that you laugh out loud for joy? I think it was that
kind of laugh. Anyway, she said she can't wait to find
out what happens.

I called George again tonight. No answer. Why do
I bother? I also spent seven minutes thinking about

Goose. That's two minutes less than last night. By the end of the summer, I'll have it down to a minute a day! And if Vince and I are together, I bet I could whittle down the time I spend obsessing over Goose to thirty seconds or less!

Wednesday, July 21
If my mother's not careful, she's going to get put in solitary confinement. Apparently, her first consciousness-raising session nearly caused a riot. I knew my mother's brand of feminism was too potent for an institutional situation. See, normally the women who take part in her this-earth-mother-ain't-gonna-take-it-anymore sessions do it outside. They run around hooting and hollering and getting in touch with their inner earth goddesses. What looks like wood nymphs having fun in a forest looks like female prisoners rioting in a jail. But that's just me reading between the lines.

Dear Alice,

We fought the patriarchy and nearly won.
But first, how are you, my darling? I was
excited to hear that your screenwriting is

going so well. I can't wait to read it! It sounds wonderful.

Anyway, as promised, I've begun consciousness-raising sessions for the other prisoners and it's just been one breakthrough after another. Marguerite (who is the western regional facilitator of the Raging Grannies) has been helping me. The things our fellow inmates have been through . . . It would break your heart. Their stories steel my resolve to be a warrior for the cause.

Samantha swears her experience in our first session wasn't just the detox talking. She got in touch with her anger and pain. Then she remembered that she was a powerful woman! We all started clapping and crying. And then dancing. It was just like the old days. So moving.

I went to the guard and asked if we could go out in the yard to celebrate. There's a tree out there that would have been perfect for a circle dance of life. But Cindy, the guard on duty, has really bought into the whole boys' club paradigm and she said no. So we staged an impromptu protest/celebration. It was incredible. All these women moving and using their voices in a non-self-destructive expression of anger. Beautiful!

I have to stay in my cell for the next two days, but that's okay because I twisted something in my back while we were dancing around the chairs we stacked in the middle of the room as a replacement tree of life.

The best part is, Samantha's boyfriend came by to visit again and she told him she'd had enough with him tromping all over her energy. Isn't that wonderful! I wasn't there, but the rumor is that he tried to attack her and was subdued by Marguerite and a few of the other women, who put him in a headlock until the guards came.

Next week's session is going to be so power-ful: I can feel it heating up already. They better let us into the yard. No meeting room is big enough to hold us!

All my love,
Your mother

Oh brother.

Actually, speaking of brothers, mine is nowhere to be found again. I guess with my father's depression and my preoccupation with employment and screenwriting there's not much around here for him to do. I mean, except for looking after his fish and performing his science experiments. I wonder if Helen's family would be interested in adopting me too?

Just kidding. But I really do need to start planning his birthday party. I want our house to be the choice destination for all the eleven-year-olds in the neighborhood. I want MacGregor to be the envy of all his friends. And most of all, I want my brother to be around so he's available for me to talk to.

Thursday, July 22
The Teens in Transition (Not in Trouble) Center was very quiet this afternoon. Normally, there are dozens of teens in transition (and quite a few in trouble) trying to get in to see Bob for unscheduled appointments. Every second female in Smithers has a crush on Bob. That might account for his high number of counseling customers. But maybe Ms. Deitrich has everyone all sorted out so they don't even *need* counseling anymore. I can just see it: high-functioning teenagers as far as the eye can see. We'll be designing buildings and achieving goals and won't have time to have problems, never mind

counseling. It's a heartwarming vision and one I'd like to be a part of.

I walked into her office, and we sat in silence for a long, long minute. Man, she is one tough customer! I practically invented stonewalling, and she was beating me at my own game.

I caved and started to babble. "Yeah, so I've been *really* busy. I'm dating again, you know. An older man. I got two jobs, so I'm working. Which is, whew! Huge." I ran a hand over my fevered brow to show just how huge.

"Plus I'm writing. And that's going great. Just great. And you remember my mom's in jail, right? Yeah, so I'm kind of in charge of the family. Which is tough. Because we're sort of going broke because my dad can't find a job. It's basically up to me to handle things around the house."

Ms. Deitrich watched me unblinkingly. "This is quite a tragedy," she said.

I modestly bowed my head. "Yeah, well."

"Tell me about this handling of things around the house."

I cleared my throat. "Well, I'm home a lot. Because my jobs are sort of part-time. So I'm there if anyone needs to talk. And I write letters to my mom in jail. To help keep up her spirits."

"Your mother, she is imprisoned for two months? For the worthy cause, yes?"

"Sure. Yeah."

"Your helping consists of writing letters and being available for talking. Is there anything else?"

I started to feel annoyed with Ms. Deitrich.

"Like?"

"Like the cleaning and cooking and contributing to the finances."

I recoiled in horror. I don't clean! Or cook! And was she seriously suggesting I give some of my hard-earned money to my family?

"Well, I'm kind of the kid in this situation," I said. "I really think it's up to my dad."

"He is trying to find the job?"

"I suppose."

"Well, there you go. Life isn't always what we want. Perhaps if you are old enough to date older men you are old enough to be useful at home," she said.

"Fine," I said, but I didn't mean it. In fact, I may have to inquire about where Ms. Deitrich got her counseling license. She may be a fraud! She certainly doesn't have the right attitude for working with young people.

Later

After a bit of consideration, I'm not quite as angry at Ms. Deitrich. In fact, there's something about her that I find comforting. She's like an island of control in a sea of chaos. Maybe she's right and it's time to step up to the plate at home. Ugh. How boring. What other sixteen-year-old has to do this—cook, clean, contribute to the finances of the household? It's exactly this kind of situation that ends up with social services involved.

A CHIP OFF THE OLD BLOCK

Friday, July 23

I was feeling so unsettled by Ms. Deitrich's challenge, I actually decided to go to martial arts practice. Not because it was a way to avoid doing housework this afternoon, but because I need the discipline.

Like I said, our teacher, Shawn, is away for the summer so the regular dojo is closed. He's in California at some summer camp for no-holds-barred fighters. I wonder if they get up in the morning, have breakfast, beat the hell out of each other all day, and then sing camp songs at night? That would be quite funny. Anyway, before he left, he told us he expects all of us, but especially the Intermediate Bees (as opposed to the Beginner Bees, or worse, the Butterflies, who are basically little kids), to practice at home every day and join the group practices in the park. If I don't improve I'm never going to become an Advanced Bee or get to join the Bears. They are the highest level in our dojo. For a tough guy, Shawn sure has lightweight names for his training levels. Anyway, as

I may have mentioned, I haven't practiced at all, and Shawn has been gone for over a month.

Part of the problem is that Jeff, the most advanced Bear in our club, is overseeing the practice sessions. I'm not trying to brag or anything, but Jeff had quite a crush on me when I first joined the Asskickers Dojo. It was one of those involuntary crushes. He didn't even like me that much. He's one of those guys who likes girls to be conventional, and he was always suggesting I should try and at least *look* a bit more normal. But the crush was a serious thing for him. And I sort of suspect that he might still have feelings. I mean, how could he get over me that fast? I told him I had a boyfriend, and the next thing you know, he was trying to pretend he was over me. Which I'm convinced he wasn't, at least not completely.

Sure, he's supposedly got this new girlfriend now. Her name's Amelia and she's not only tough, but also quite normal and average and all that. Jeff and Amelia are running the "informal practice sessions." I haven't gone because I don't want to stir anything up, if you know what I mean. But I figure it's time for Jeff to get over his lingering feelings of love for me. Also, I need to show up at practice at least once before

Shawn comes back or I'm going to get demoted and end up back with the little kids.

I walked up to where they were practicing in the park, and Jeff, who has clearly gone power-mad since he started leading the group, said, "Well, look at this! Where have *you* been?"

I informed him that I've been busy—work, family, screenplays, etc.—and he said, "Well, you better spar with one of the kids so you don't get hurt." Then he pointed at a Butterfly who was practically an infant.

So I said, "Shut up," but in a respectful way, and then told him that I've been practicing on my own, practically every day. "I'm probably almost ready to advance to the Bears."

"Okay," he said doubtfully, and then paired me up with his girlfriend, Amelia.

I used to spar with Melinda. She's Shawn's girl-friend and is about a million times tougher than I am, but we were in the Miss Smithers Pageant together last winter so I could count on her to take it easy on me. But Melinda was off at the training camp with Shawn. I tried to be very gentle with Amelia, you know, emotionally, in case I made her feel jealous or insecure just from my presence.

Amelia moved to Smithers a couple of months ago from Burns Lake. She's brown-haired and pleasant. And, as it turns out, she has a hidden jealous streak and a wicked right hook, as evidenced by the HUGE CHIP missing from my front tooth!

That's right. Sweet little Amelia almost knocked out my front tooth during martial arts practice.

We went through our kata routines and then it was time to spar. When she said, "Aren't you going to put in your mouth guard?" I didn't feel like telling her I'd forgotten it, so I said, "Nah. I doubt you're going to get close enough to hit me. I've been training at the dojo for quite a while."

How was I supposed to know she'd been studying karate since she was five?

Her first punch hit me in the face, and I thought I heard a cracking sound. I immediately covered my mouth with my gloved hands and made a groaning noise.

"Oh my god!" cried Amelia. "I'm so sorry."

I just love these people who knock out your teeth and then get all girlish and apologetic about it.

From behind my hands, I tried to say, "My tooth," but it came out "Mmmffff."

Jeff, who has the martial artist's antenna for violence, was at our side in an instant.

"What's going on here?"

"I hit her," confessed Amelia.

"I told you to take it easy on her," he said.

"She practically walked into my hand. And she refused to put in her mouth guard."

Jeff tried to get me to drop my hands so he could look at my mouth, but I shook my head.

"Come on. Let me see."

I could sense everyone around us trying to listen in.

"It's probably just a fat lip," said Jeff. This was apparently supposed to make me feel better.

Already feeling very sorry for myself, I lowered my hands and opened my mouth.

Amelia looked closely in my mouth.

"I don't see anything," she said.

"Are you sure?"

"Did you always have that little chip out of your front tooth?"

"——!!" I gasped.

"You can't even see it," said Jeff.

"Is there blood?" I asked. "Am I bleeding?"

"No. You just have a tiny chip out of your tooth."

"I can't look. Is it bad?"

"No, it's not bad. It's just, I don't know. Chipped."

I clamped my mouth shut again.

Amelia, Jeff, and the rest of the Asskickers walked with me to the edge of the park. "It's just a chip," said Amelia, trying to make me feel better. "They can easily fix that. Some fighters lose whole teeth."

Later
Other fighters may lose entire teeth. But those other fighters probably have a dental plan. It turns out we don't, and my dad just informed me that to get my tooth fixed would cost "more than we've got right now. Besides, you can't even notice it."

How do you like that? I am going to look like this until I can find a job with a dental plan. And I have a date tomorrow with someone I really like!

Many screenwriters may be plain and slightly unkempt, but I'd be willing to bet money they have perfect teeth.

This is horrible. I don't know how I can face Vince. Oh well, at least his teeth aren't the last word in perfection.

It goes without saying that with the tooth issue and all, I wasn't able to pitch in around the house tonight, although I did pat Mac on the back when I saw him doing the dishes. Since Finn and Devlin came over and Devlin cooked dinner and Finn helped Mac do the dishes, I really feel like my presence wasn't required. I have enough on my mind, what with my date coming up tomorrow and all.

OF MOOSE AND MEN
A SCREENPLAY BY ALICE MACLEOD

ACT II
SCENE 2:
FADE IN.
MOUNTAINOUS AREA—EVENING

Quietly attractive, outdoorsy-looking GIRL emerges from a tent. Her blond braids swing in the clean mountain air as she surveys the landscape. She is like a wild creature, attuned to the environment. She thinks she is all alone. There is a feeling of suspense in the air, which makes the scene quite thrilling.

*Suddenly, there is a noise in
the brush. The GIRL turns with
catlike reflexes.*

GIRL

Who's there?

*A MAN emerges from the shrubs.
He is carrying a piece of
paper.*

GIRL

   (In a tense, catlike voice)
Who are you? What are you doing
in these mountains?

MAN

I am here on behalf of Quentin
Tarantino. He is working on a
new film. He needs a female
lead. Someone with the soul of
a cat and the heart of a lion.
He immediately thought of you.
Also, he needs help with the
writing.

GIRL

*(Turns her head, sadly and
with a lot of grace.)*
I can't.

MAN

But why? It's the role of
a lifetime! It's a Quentin
Tarantino project. It will be
a cult hit and achieve popular
acclaim!

GIRL

(A sob in her feline voice)
It's just everything. I have
a duty to my family. And the
children. And then there's this
thing about me that you don't
know ...

(Tense silence)

MAN

What thing?

GIRL

(Blond braids swinging sadly in
    time with her shaking head)
I can't say.

MAN

But you must.

GIRL

(Bravely turns to him and shows
    her teeth. It's an incredible
    moment. Like when a tiger
snarls. Frightening and thrill-
    ing all at the same time.)

MAN

You mean the sexy chip in your
tooth?

GIRL

(Head hanging in dejection)
Yes.

MAN

You silly, silly little star.

That's what the part calls for:
a sexy, catlike woman with a
small chip out of her tooth.
If you didn't have the chip,
the special effects department
would have had to make one!
Your chip just makes you even
more perfect!

*GIRL's face registers surprise
and joy.*

FADE OUT.

CATCH AND RELEASE

Saturday, July 24

Vince showed up right on time. In a car! I looked out my window, alerted by rumbling noises, to see an old, rust-pocked Ford Tempo idling in our driveway.

I watched as he turned off the car and sat forward so his forehead rested on the steering wheel. Then he sat up abruptly, opened the door, and got out. His outfit showed no signs that we were headed for the outdoors. He wore exactly the same jeans, runners, and T-shirt as always.

Wearing my golf outfit and vintage saddle shoes (no practical Interview Shoes for me on my big date!), I raced downstairs so he wouldn't knock and wake up my dad. For a fleeting moment I was grateful that my mom wasn't home to give him the third degree and invite him in for organic oatmeal.

"Hi!" I whispered breathlessly, keeping my lips pulled tight over my chip as I opened the front door.

"Hi."

"Let's go." I pushed him out the door.

I got in the passenger seat of the Tempo, not waiting for him to open the door for me. Then I looked up at the house to see if MacGregor or my dad was watching out the window and was relieved to see they weren't.

The car was old. It smelled like perishable things had been left under the seats. The interior was covered with a fine layer of dust.

"So you got your license back," I congratulated him.

Hands on the steering wheel of the parked, silent car, Vince looked straight ahead.

"Not exactly."

"Sorry?"

"Well, it's just so hard to, you know, get anywhere. It's only a few weeks till I get my license back. It shouldn't matter."

Whoa. No license. "Are you sure this is a good idea?" I said, distracted from my worry by the need to keep my front tooth hidden. Then another thought occurred to me.

"Whose car is this?"

I was relieved to hear him say it was his cousin's. At least he didn't steal it.

He added, "Anyway, it's six thirty. No one's going to

stop us. It's cool. Sometimes you just—" He stopped. "Hey, what's going on? Why is your mouth all puckered up like that?"

I looked at him like I didn't know what he was talking about.

"Oh, come on. Did you go to the dentist yesterday?"

"I wish," I muttered.

"So what's up?"

I rolled my eyes and bared my teeth at him. "Ith thipped," I said, pointing in case he couldn't see the piece missing.

"I think I see it," he said, staring intently. "Kinda cute," he said. "Goes with the crazy clothes."

Needless to say I didn't bring up the whole no-license thing again. I didn't want to make him feel bad by questioning his judgment. After all, he was twenty-two. He knew what he was doing. And he liked my chip. And my golfing outfit.

When Vince finally started the car it erupted into a series of explosive backfires and then the engine began to make slightly irregular *putt, putt . . . putt* noises, like a dune buggy in need of a tune-up.

"Is this car okay? I mean, how far are we going?"

"Not too far. We'll make it." He cast a glance over at my clothes. "Or we can just ride your golf cart if we break down."

Behind me a large backpack lay across the backseat. It was covered with attachments: cylindrical cases, straps, and buckles that connected to baby backpacks. Where were we going? Dinner at the Lodge and walking around the Perimeter Trail was one thing. Going into the bush in a broken-down old car accompanied by a bag big enough to hold my dismembered body was another thing. Suddenly, I wished I hadn't rushed out of the house quite so fast. Did my dad even know where I was?

I stole a look at Vince and saw that his hair was still wet and his skin had that slightly raw look that comes from shaving. Then I felt nervous and bad for him too.

"So you like hiking, eh?" he said. I could see him staring at the pack of cigarettes on the dashboard and knew he wanted one but wouldn't have it while I was in the car.

"Sure. Yeah," I replied, trying to work some enthusiasm into my voice.

"So you must love your new job. All that hiking."

I nodded, thinking that my lie about hiking was

going to snowball until I found myself signed up for an Everest expedition.

Vince pulled the car into a gravel parking lot with a wooden check-in stand at the entrance to the trail.

Removing the key from the ignition, he turned to me and seemed about to say something. Then he thought the better of it and just shrugged and got out.

I stood beside the car and watched him. He was such a contradiction: long hair, eyes squinting from the unlit cigarette he had clenched in his teeth, pulling with all his might to get a backpack bigger than he was out of the least outdoorsy car in the entire Northern Interior.

He finally wrenched the bag free and hoisted it up onto his back like a Bulgarian powerlifter in the final round of the Olympics. It looked like it weighed more than he did and he stumbled back and forth a few steps before catching his balance.

"Can I take something?" I asked.

"No, I'm good," he said. "We're not going that far. I've got it balanced just so."

The load didn't look balanced. The things he'd tied to the pack shifted from side to side with every step he took, banging into one another. The lower-slung items drooped farther and farther down and by the time we reached the trail they were bashing into the backs of his knees.

"You sure I can't take anything?"

"No. I'm a finely tuned machine here. Don't want to mess up the alignment."

He was already puffing from the walk across the parking lot.

"I friggin' love hiking," he said, staggering onto the trail without stopping at the sign-in station.

"Don't you want to put our names down for the ranger? You know, in case we get lost?"

"Can't stop," he called back to me. "Don't want to lose momentum," he gasped and disappeared around the bend.

I quickly filled out the form and hurried after him.

I don't love hiking. In fact, I think I hate it. Short walks, preferably to a clothing store, are acceptable. I'd probably enjoy leisurely strolls along a boulevard somewhere in France, and spring jaunts down Fifth Avenue in New York. But long, grueling mountain treks in British Columbia do not appeal to me. So why was I spending practically every minute of my summer doing them?

Even though I didn't have to carry anything I started to complain mentally after going about three feet. Feelings of pity for poor license-less Vince gave way to feelings of pity for poor, overworked Alice. We were probably headed for some high alpine lake that stayed frozen year-round due to the elevation. No, scratch that. We were probably headed for a glacier. Vince was going to take me ice climbing, which, with my luck, would prove fatal. At least with the Backpackers Club I got paid for this kind of thing.

The trees loomed overhead. I could sense bears and mountain lions watching me. I was alone and about to be mauled by a multitude of wild creatures. They'd probably take turns. First the bears would eat my face. Then the wolves would eat my insides. The crows would take the rest. Waste not, want not. Isn't that the motto of the wild kingdom?

The pain in my feet and the ache in my back didn't take my mind off my fear at all. Then the path started to climb. Panicky thoughts spun through my head. *I can't do this! I'm not going to make it!*

Relief joined embarrassment when I rounded the bend and found Vince leaning against a tree. The pack sat at his feet. Behind him was an opening in the trees, revealing a river with a sandy bank.

"You enjoy that?" he asked.

I made a noncommittal noise.

"Well, that's the longest hike you'll ever take with me." It turned out that the giant pack contained everything needed for a relaxing day on the river. Vince dragged it over to where some logs lay at the high-water mark. He unpacked two folding chairs, a small barbecue, a cooler designed to fit in the bottom of the pack, two fishing rods, bear spray, bug spray, and a first aid kit.

He set up the chairs on the sandy riverbank.

"You sit here," he said. "Okay. Now relax." He handed me a compact blanket.

After rustling around some more he appeared beside my chair with a fishing rod.

"Hang onto this. If you get a bite, reel it in."

I looked at him doubtfully.

"Like this." He grabbed the rod and showed me.

For a supposedly earthy family we spend almost no time outdoors. I was amazed at how enjoyable it was sitting there watching the river slide by, listening to the birds, and the reassuring sounds of Vince setting up camp behind me. I looked back every so often and realized that he was in cook mode. He had the tiny barbecue perched on a log and a coffee pot on a propane burner.

"You need any help?" I called back to him.

"No. I've got it."

He sat down in the chair beside me and leaned his rod against it, pausing only for a moment. "You good?"

I nodded, not even trying to hide my chip because this was all so cool.

"Good," he said, satisfied, and disappeared again.

Soon, the most amazing smells began to waft past me. I kept sneaking looks but his concentration never wavered. He was the total professional, intent on his work.

He came over and fit a cup of coffee into the holder in the armrest of my chair.

"Cream and sugar, right?"

"How'd you know?"

"I see stuff." He tapped himself in the temple. "Smart."

Then he directed me to reel in my line.

I put my rod down, and he handed me a plate with sausages and scrambled eggs and toast and half a grilled tomato.

"This looks amazing," I said, afraid to tell him that I don't eat meat.

"Veggie sausages," he announced. "You *are* vegetarian, right?"

I nodded gratefully.

"Well, eat up. We've got some sitting to do."

We sat side by side, warmed by the sun. The flavors of the food seemed heightened in the morning air. I could feel the dark heat of the coffee as it moved down my throat into my stomach.

When we were done, Vince wouldn't even let me clean up. He whisked away the plates and the rest of the dishes disappeared into the pack and then he poured us some more coffee and put our fishing lines in the water.

He seemed happy not to talk, and I was in such a state of contentment I couldn't think of anything that needed to be said. When we did start to talk it was almost unnoticeable. One minute I was thinking and the next I was speaking. Which is not to say we had one of those longtime-couple mind-reading conversations like my parents have. It was just this very nice, casual conversation.

We were just talking about talent and how you know you have one and how you know you don't, when there was a tug on my line. I'd almost forgotten we were fishing and in my shock I nearly dropped the rod and almost fell out of my chair.

"Hold on!" Vince said. "Hold it up!"

The tip jerked again and I screamed.

Vince steadied my hand.

Excitement and a kind of horror followed as I brought the fish in, its silver body rising in protest and then diving again, pulling hard.

"Easy. Easy. Just reel it in. You got him," Vince whispered.

When he knelt at the water's edge to lift the fish from the water, I was amazed to see how small it was. It felt like a dolphin on the end of my line, but it wasn't much bigger than my two hands.

"You want to keep him?"

"No, no thanks," I said, almost sickened at the idea.

Then I knelt beside him and watched as he tried to pull the hook out of the fish's bony mouth.

"Can you get me my pliers?" he asked. "The hook's stuck."

Panicking a bit, I ran and found a small pair of yellow-handled pliers in the tackle box beside Vince's chair and rushed to hand them to him.

He breathed hard as he worked, his brown hands moving, trying to dislodge the hook without touching the fish too much. Vince made a noise deep in his throat when he finally got the hook free. Keeping the fish in swimming position, he moved its body from side to side and back and forth in the water until it slid from his hands and disappeared with a small splash into the main current of the river.

We both stayed at the water's edge as Vince washed his hands. His running shoes and bottoms of his jeans were wet. When he stood up, sweat or maybe river water gleamed on his forehead. And when I stood up and kissed him his tongue went right to the chip in my tooth.

SAY ANYTHING BUT THAT

Sunday, July 25

I am a screenwriter and therefore have an open mind and expect the unexpected. But I didn't expect the conversation I just had with Vince.

On the way home yesterday I was completely in love or, at least, in total like. So much so that I didn't notice that Vince had been behaving strangely ever since I kissed him. I was so happy I didn't think anything of it when he asked when I was turning seventeen. I was so happy when I got home I barely reacted when my dad asked about eight hundred questions about our date: What did Vince and I do? Where did we go? How old was Vince again?

I was actually impressed that Dad was able to struggle through his depression, which seems to be getting worse every day he goes without working, enough to meddle in my personal life.

I was incredibly excited when Vince called this morning at 9:03. I thought it showed commitment and eagerness.

"Hi, Alice."

"Oh hi!"

"Is this too early?"

"No, not at all," I said, trying to keep the just-woke-up sound out of my voice.

"Ha," he said, but there was no real amusement in his voice. "Look, I have to talk to you about something."

"What?" Here it comes. A confession of undying love. Or maybe an offer to go steady.

"I don't know if this is going to work out."

"What?"

"I really like you. You have no idea. But you're sixteen. I'm twenty-two. It just doesn't feel right. And to be honest, I can't handle feeling wrong anymore."

"What?"

"I just feel like . . . I feel like an old pervert or something. It's like you're this nice girl and I'm this, you know, cook with an impaired charge, and you can't even get into a bar. If you were just a couple years older . . . I just don't think I can handle it."

"But, I thought—"

"I'm sorry. You have no idea how sorry I am."

"But—"

"Take care, Alice."

And then he hung up!

What the hell is that? I don't want to go all low self-esteem about it, but maybe he finally noticed that I'm not traditionally attractive. Or maybe he gave it some thought and he can't be with someone who has dental issues.

Later

I've watched *Say Anything* twice since Vince called, but it's not helping. I just don't have what it takes to go and camp outside Vince's house and serenade him with a boom box. For one thing, our boom box is really big and old and I don't think I could even get it to knee level, never mind lift it up over my head like Lloyd did. Also, I have no idea where Vince lives.

I know! I'll look him up in the phone book!

2:05 P.M.

I just realized I don't know Vince's last name. We've had two dates. I really should know his last name. How am I going to practice writing my married name over and over if I don't even know his name?

Mrs.????

Mrs. Vince ???

Mrs. Married to Vince.

Maybe I could go feminist. He could be:

Mr. Alice MacLeod.

Or we could be:

Mr. and Dr. MacLeod.

Ha! My mother would like that.

But seriously. This is no joke. I've got to find out how to reach him and let him know he's made a terrible mistake.

2:15 P.M.

I just called Karen. She thinks his last name is Selby. Luckily, there are only seven Selbys in the Smithers phone book.

2:18 P.M.

I kind of have a thing about calling wrong numbers. What if he is the last Selby in the book? I don't think I can bring myself to call six wrong numbers. I don't think I'm cut out for phone stalking.

2:56 P.M.

I just borrowed MacGregor's skateboard and rode by the Number Four. I looked in the window as I went by, trying to see if Vince was working. Unfortunately, I wiped out just as I passed the restaurant and wound up hitting a parked car and banging my head. Fortunately, I didn't damage any more teeth.

I've informed my dad that I'll be in bed until tomorrow. This is probably dangerous due to my mild concussion, but I'm simply too depressed to remain upright.

Dad asked what was wrong, but didn't have the energy to pursue it when I said, "Nothing." In fact, he said if I need anything he'd be in bed also. MacGregor asked if we needed anything before he went to Helen's. I got him to make me a hot chocolate. I want to make him feel useful. Our family really is on the verge of disintegration.

7:38 P.M.
I got up briefly to write the following e-mail to Goose:

> *Dear Goose,*
>
> *I know we aren't talking. But I was just think-ing about you. Not because things are going badly for me or anything. I was thinking about that time you showed up at the Sweetheart*

Ball, late, as usual. I'd given up on you, but then, right at the end, you showed up. I've just been thinking about that lately.

Anyway, I hope things are good in Scotland. And if you are still seeing your new Swedish friend, I'm glad for you but don't really want to know about it.

I miss you.

Love,
Alice
(P.S. Do they have moose in Scotland?)

Even though I deleted the message right away, somehow writing it made me feel better.

Monday, July 26

I'm up. I'm up. Nothing like fifteen hours in bed to make a person feel worse.

I promised to help Betty Lou today so I have to get dressed. The only positive thing I can think of now is that I'm going to be quite rich because I'm due to get paid by Betty Lou and the Bulkley Valley Junior Backpackers soon. If I play my cards right I could be a hundred-aire by the end of the summer.

Later

When I walked into the shop, which is now crammed full of boxes, Betty Lou was nowhere to be seen.

I was just about to feel some yarn when a door leading to the shop next door opened and Betty Lou slipped through.

"Oh. Hi, Alice. You're here." She sounded surprised.

"Reporting for duty. As requested."

Betty Lou seemed a bit disheveled. In her radical street sort of way she's usually immaculate. Not a tattoo out of place. Bobbed helmet with precise black bangs. But now she looked like she'd just gotten dressed in a hurry. Maybe it was because she was unpacking.

"Right," she said, smoothing down her black T-shirt with the skull and crossbones as though she'd just put it on. "Could I get you to finish making labels for the shelves? I've got the list and the stickers right here."

For a while we worked in silence. Then I found myself telling her that I'd just been dumped. Again.

"The older guy?" she asked.

"Yeah. He said he was too old. Or I was too young. Something like that."

Betty Lou shook her head. "Oh, a *mature* older guy."

I nodded. "You wouldn't think it. You know, to look at him."

She turned her black-rimmed eyes to me.

"I'm just saying," I clarified.

"Right," she said.

And even though we were sort of on shaky ground, I volunteered a bit more information about the pressures at home. If I was hoping to get a different answer from her than from Ms. Deitrich, I was out of luck.

"So you don't want to help out?"

"It's not that I don't want to. It's just that I'm, like, busy. I've got two jobs. And, you know, I'm writing a lot."

"Some people have to help out around the house because their parents are total deadbeats: drug addicts, alcoholics. Around my house, man, you either did or you did without. First my older sister did it. After she bolted, I took over."

"Where were your parents?"

"Parent," she corrected. "The old man was drunk off his ass all the time until he did us all a favor and left. And Mom was, shall we say, a bit intermittent in her parenting."

I didn't know what to say.

"I moved out and got married when I was seventeen. Figured I was escaping. Turns out I just started looking after somebody new."

"You were married before?"

"Nothing like a trip to Vegas to make a bad idea reality." Betty Lou laughed in her raspy way. "The worst six months of my life."

"Look, Alice," she continued. "It's none of my business. But you said your dad's trying to get a job. Your mom's in jail, doing her thing. And your brother's awesome. He's so gold he's practically Ponyboy. It could be worse."

Ugh. There it was again. No one has any sympathy for me. Sure, Betty Lou has had a hard life. Some kids, in some places, have to do everything. *But I don't want to!*

Instead of shaming me further, Betty Lou asked if I was ready to learn to knit. And because I'm afraid of her, instead of sulking, I said yes. We were about to start the lesson when the door between the store and the Eternal Anchor swung open and a man walked through.

He looked how I imagined Goose's Glasgwegian hooligans did. Dangerous. His hair was cropped so short he was almost bald, and he wore a white T-shirt and plain black pants. His arms were covered in tattoos and he had pointy sideburns.

"Betty Lou," he said, "you forgot something."

Then he handed her something black and see-through.

Oh my god! Betty Lou was cheating on Bob with a tough guy who was covered in tattoos! Bob may dye his hair black but otherwise he's a sensitive New-Age teen-counselor guy. This was terrible news. Betty Lou's moral compass must have been damaged by her terrible upbringing! She didn't know right from wrong! She was going to hurt Bob!

I looked wildly around, trying not to see what was so totally obvious.

My counselor, Bob, was a cuckold!

My next reaction was disapproval, which was followed by a surge of loyal feeling. Never mind that Betty Lou gave me a job and was trying to be nice to me and came from the school of hard knocks. She was cheating on *my* counselor. Nobody messes with Bob but me. I try to give him a professional challenge by messing with his head, but I would never mess with anyone's whole heart.

I considered storming out after delivering a brief but

pointed lecture in chastity. But then I thought about how I needed the job. And about Betty Lou getting married when she was only a year older than me.

I solved the problem of what to do by pretending I hadn't seen anything.

I don't want to know this, I prayed silently. *I don't want to see this.*

No such luck.

"Alice, this is Kyle. He works next door at the Anchor."

Keeping my gaze trained on the floor, I said, "Hi."

"Hey, there," came the masculine voice.

"Alice is helping me get set up. She might even work here part-time when we're up and running."

"Cool," said the man-voice. "I'll see you later."

And the door closed, leaving us alone. Betty Lou acted as though nothing had happened, as though I hadn't just busted her, practically in the act of betraying my counselor.

"So you ready to learn to cast on?"

"I just remembered I have to be somewhere."

"Oh. Okay. Well, I guess I can show you next time."

"Great," I said and hustled out of the store, head whirling. This was the woman I'd been asking for relationship advice!

OF MOOSE AND MEN
A SCREENPLAY BY ALICE MACLEOD

ACT II
SCENE 3:
FADE IN.
YARN STORE INTERIOR ON
FILM SET—DAY

Artistic-looking GIRL enters
film set. She is obviously
involved in some aspect of
filmmaking because she is wear-
ing a baseball hat and black
coat. In spite of this attire,
she still manages to be very
attractive.
She looks around her. She is
looking for something. She
spots a YOUNG MAN.

GIRL

Have you seen Quentin?

YOUNG MAN

Oh my god. Miss Marseilles! It's
such an honor to meet the mind
behind this amazing film project.
And also the lead actress.

GIRL

(Humbly)
You are too kind. Please.
*(Her voice, as well as sound-
ing like a combination of some
French person and J.Lo, also
has an undercurrent of Meryl
Streep. You can tell that the
GIRL is practically a chameleon
when it comes to accents.)*
I need to find Quentin
Tarantino. I have a question
about the script. I've come
down off the mountain to do
this role and I feel I must
give it my all.

YOUNG MAN
(*Breathlessly*)
But of course, Miss Marseilles.
It's an honor just to meet you,
never mind give you directions.

There is a rustling behind the
set. The young man strides over
and opens a door. There is
Quentin Tarantino in a shocking
position with ANOTHER WOMAN!

GIRL
I am shocked!

QUENTIN TARANTINO
Annette! I . . . I . . .

GIRL
Please, you don't even have to
say it. You've given away my
role to another woman. The role
I left the mountain for. Even
though I helped you write the

screenplay about the drama that
takes place in a yarn store.

YOUNG MAN
(*Speaking to the audience
in a low voice, like one of
Shakespeare's chorus*)
This is a tragedy. A travesty.
It's just plain wrong.

GIRL
(*Sadly*)
I won't let this make me jaded
about the film industry.

*She walks out with her usual
feline dignity and grace. As
she's about to leave the stage
set, she turns.*

GIRL
I still believe in love and
honor.

QUENTIN TARANTINO
(To himself)

I've destroyed this film! I've
destroyed my life. And now
Annette Marseilles will disappear to the mountains again.
Perhaps never to be seen in a
knitting film again.

*(Sad music. Maybe something by
the Palace Brothers.)*

FADE OUT.

I'm left a bit breathless by the sudden twists and turns in *Of Moose and Men*. My only concern is that it's becoming a bit autobiographical. But you know what they say: Write what you know!

With so much creative energy flowing, I was tempted to write an e-mail to Goose. But I stopped myself. Then I was tempted to write a letter to Vince. But through an impressive act of will I settled for a letter to my mother in which I reminded her about MacGregor's birthday. Not to get her advice, because my mother always insists on party killers like whole-wheat-flour birthday cakes and organic apple juice with all the lumps, but because I wanted to make sure she remembered his birthday. You never know what kind of effect her prison experiences might have had on her ability to remember her offsprings' birth dates. If she's hanging around with drug addicts and getting put in solitary, she could be disoriented. Also, I'm hoping that she might have a stash of money hidden somewhere that I could use to help pay for the party.

Then I spent the rest of the evening getting ready for the hike tomorrow. The reason I care about my outfit is not because I want to impress anyone. I've been disappointed in love twice this summer. It's obvious that I'm destined to be single and will never have sex. That's fine. I can live with that. But Evan had warned me that we're "taking the kids fishing" and to "dress appropriately."

I think the right clothes might help me get in touch with my outdoorsy self. Some people hardly think about the wilderness, even though they live in Smithers and are surrounded by it. But not me. Ever since that time in the car with Goose, I long for the rugged mountains, the cloud-scudded skies, and end-less expanses of pine trees. And since that day I spent with Vince, I'm quite into raging rivers. I may not want to *walk around* in the wilderness *per se*, but that doesn't mean I don't appreciate it on a deeper level than the average person.

In order to project the right image, not just for Evan but also for the children, after the first hike I had asked my dad to buy me some hiking gear. MacGregor showed me all my options on the Mountain Equipment Co-op website. The male models alone were enough to confirm my commitment to the great outdoors. But due to our extreme poverty Dad said no to every single one of my requests. It was completely unfair. I don't see how one pair of Italian leather hiking boots, two pairs of special "Smart Socks," pants with legs that zip off so they convert into shorts, a hat with a North Face logo and detachable face netting, a silk undershirt that "wicks away moisture," and one of those made-specially-for-women backpacks that expands from the size of a piece of toast to the size of a Volkswagen Bug is going to make much difference to our finances.

"Get serious, Alice," said Dad after I read off the list. "You can use MacGregor's stuff. You're just going for a short hike, not through the Khumbu Ice Fields."

"Yeah," I whined, "but everyone says you have to be prepared. It's my job to be prepared."

"So bring some Band-Aids," he snapped, losing patience.

All I have to say is that if something happens to me on this hike he'll have to live with it. It's not a responsibility I'd want.

A MILE IN SOMEONE ELSE'S CLUB-FOOT BOOTS

Wednesday, July 28

I ended up wearing castoffs that belong to members of my family (not to be confused with interesting thrift-store clothes). Last night I tried explaining to my father that 95 percent of fitting into any setting is looking the part, but he was unmoved. For instance, if a person wants to go on a sailboat, she needs Jackie O sunglasses, a navy-and-white-striped T-shirt, and canvas deck shoes. (This is minimum, mind you). Otherwise, she'll look like a deckhand and won't have a good time. I know this from reading magazines.

Likewise, if a person is going on a hiking/fishing trip, she needs to look right. I don't look right, and it just might cost me my job. I'd imagine that my father's willful refusal to grasp this concept has made him the unemployable person he is today.

To avoid a skin-damaging burn, the effects of which might hurt my ability to play the youthful female lead in a play or film, I'm wearing my dad's floppy, white, fake Tilley fishing hat, the same one he uses to go horseback riding. I've been forced to wear my own pants, a pair of army cargos that I was bored with months ago. And for a backpack I have the little one MacGregor got as a gift with subscription to *Owl* magazine. On my feet I've got Mother's hideous twenty-year-old hiking boots, which were apparently inspired by the design of a Dutch clog and look as though they were made specially for someone with two club feet.

Not exactly groundbreaking outdoorswear.

I wonder if Evan will be able to see past my scraggly outerwear to the amazing person within. Goose could, but that doesn't do me much good now that he lives in Scotland and is probably engaged to a Swedish supermodel. And Vince is afraid to see beneath the surface, due to me being too young. Or something like that.

Later

According to their pamphlet, the Bulkley Valley Junior Backpackers Club is an organization devoted to teaching youth how to "safely experience the great outdoors." Junior Backpackers are taught orienteering and wilderness safety. They learn the local trail systems and are also introduced to a variety of

197

healthy outdoor activities, such as fly fishing, photography, back country camping and, in winter, Nordic skiing and avalanche awareness. They are taught these things by "skilled guide/counselors" and parent volunteers. And for this privilege, the Backpackers' parents pay hundreds of dollars.

I don't want to sound paranoid, but if I were a parent hoping to make my child into the next Grizzly Adams, I might be concerned if I thought he or she was being taught by a girl in an *Owl* backpack and club-foot boots. For this reason, I lingered at the side of the parking lot this morning while the Backpackers were dropped off.

Ted found me almost instantly, possibly using one of his devices. He may be the youngest of my three hiking protégés, but he's undoubtedly the most competent in the wilderness arena. "Why are you hiding back here?" he asked.

"What?" I said; then, because I am a guide/counselor, I pretended to be searching the underbrush with my club-foot boot.

"What are you looking for?" asked Renée, who'd followed Ted.

"Nothing, just, you know, some foliage. A very interesting type found in this, um, habitat."

"You mean near outhouses?" asked Ted and Renée together.

That explained the smell.

I reluctantly followed them into the parking lot, where Evan greeted me.

"Hey hon," he said.

Hon! Short for honey! He almost called me honey!

Like many gorgeous and fit people, Evan seems always on the verge of bursting into laughter, presumably over the good fortune that made him so perfect. I managed to work a smile onto my face to mask my shock that the best-looking man in the world had just called me a synonym for sweet!

"You're all geared out today, eh?" he said.

Renée and Ted made faces, and I tried to pretend I felt completely confident in my non-guide-approved clothing.

Evan gestured for me to follow him.

"We're walking up the logging road to Battleship Lake, and there we're going to fly fish. Have you fished before?"

I thought back to my day with Vince. He did everything except hold the rod, but it was still technically fishing. "Oh, here and there," I said, trying to be vague enough so he wouldn't develop expectations about my fishing abilities but would still be impressed with my well-roundedness.

"Right. So I'll give the general lesson and then you'll help the kids in your group get set up and cast."

"And the hike?" I asked anxiously. "How long is the hike?"

"Oh, not far. Maybe an hour and a half. I'm driving up with the equipment and you and Jeanine can walk up with the kids."

We were interrupted by her royal heartiness, Jeanine, who said, "That's not too far for you, is it? I mean, after all, you've got your *Owl* backpack to carry."

I glared at her.

"Evan felt you and your team might need some extra help," she said, undeterred by my rudeness.

Even though Evan is completely out of my league in all recognizable ways (i.e., in looks, attitude, physical fitness), I found myself feeling a bit jealous and competitive.

"You just worry about your own team," I said. "Me and my guys don't need any help."

My guys? Did I just call my small band of weirdos "my guys"? When did I turn into Staff Sergeant MacLeod?

Just then Wallace arrived. He flung himself out of

a yellow Mercedes piloted by his father, who wore a brilliant pink golf shirt. In the passenger seat sat his mother, and I could see her dismayed, red-lipsticked mouth from across the parking lot. Wallace was, as usual, dressed all in black and his eyeliner was as liberally applied as his mother's lipstick. He slouched past us, face set in a dramatic scowl.

"Fishing," he griped as he stormed past. "Probably in some alpine lake. Are fish safe nowhere?"

His mother got halfway out of the car. She waved hesitantly and called across to him. "Wally? Wally, sweetie? Your lunch."

Wallace ignored his mother, and Renée walked over to collect the backpack.

"Have you met Mr. and Mrs. Landsdowne yet?" Jeanine asked me.

I shook my head, then asked, "Isn't Wallace's dad a logger?"

"He's *the* logger. He owns mills from here to Prince Rupert. Mr. Landsdowne gives us about 5,000 dollars a year. Evan wouldn't let Wallace in the club otherwise. There've been a few *incidents*."

Wallace's mother was still waving out the car window as the Mercedes tore out of the parking lot in a shower of gravel and dust.

"Yeah, I can see your team is in great shape," commented Jeanine as we watched Wallace refuse to take the backpack from Renée.

"Hasn't your work visa run out yet?" I asked, but in a friendly sort of way.

Later

After climbing a trail with a grade steep enough to prevent my "team" from bickering too much, we reached our destination.

Gasping and with shaking legs, the three kids and I stumbled into the clearing. Short, jagged trees marked the edge of the forest behind us, and in front of us the silver-and-purple mountain stretched up to meet the sky. In the middle of this vista was a black lake, a perfect pool of spilled ink. Evan stood in front of the lake, and it was hard to decide what was more beautiful: the setting or him.

With his curly golden hair peeking out from under his baseball cap, brown skin soaking up the sunlight, eyes hidden behind mirrored sunglasses, and an intriguing expanse of manly neck visible under his light-purple flannel shirt, Evan was like Abercrombie and Fitch's version of a fly-fishing guide. He was how a fishing guide should look. In other words, he was hot.

We were the last ones to arrive, and Evan smiled as we walked up. I caught myself wondering why it took me so long to discover fly fishing. I could tell already that I really liked it.

The other backpackers were spread out in pairs, reading a photocopied handout.

Evan joined us.

"Hey." He stared at each of us in turn from behind his wraparound shades, his gaze finally coming to rest on me. I could see my reflection, warped and misshapen, in his glasses.

Finally, Evan pulled off his hat, ran a hand over his hair, and pushed his sunglasses up onto his head, giving us the full blue-eyed treatment. Again, I found myself thinking how much I probably love fly fishing.

"Remind me which of you have fly fished before."

Renée shook her head no. Ted volunteered that he had once, with his dad.

"Last year. With you," said Wallace with zero enthusiasm.

I shrugged and smiled and nodded all at the same time.

I noticed that Evan's eyes were a bit glassy as he slid his shades back into place.

"You guys are going to totally dig this," he said.

Then he handed each of us a few sheets of paper. "Read these, and then we're going to go over the basics of fly casting. I'll be back in a sec," he said and went to answer another group's questions.

The three sheets of text were titled "The Art of Fly Fishing Made Easy."

"Oh, no," grumbled Wallace, "not the art again."

He read aloud:

> *The purpose of the class is to help you develop the skills you will need to catch trout on a fly, including theory, rigging, casting, knots, and stream ettiquete, as well as wading safety, trout behavior, entomology, reading the water, and developing techniques to fish nymphs, dry flies, and streamers, and how to play and release your fish.*

The handout showed some smudgy images labeled CADDIS FLY, MAYFLY, DRAGONFLY, STONE FLY, and CHORONOMID. Other blurred images showed a small figure lashing something with a long whip. This was labeled FLY CASTING.

"Any questions here?" Evan inquired, rejoining our group.

"How do you spell 'etiquette'?" asked Wallace innocently.

Evan unleashed his smile. "P-O-L-I-T-E."

I laughed, impressed, and even Wallace looked chastened.

"Um, I can't tell the difference between the caddis fly and the mayfly," said Ted, who likes to make the effort.

Evan knelt down. "Well, they are both small, and they are both bugs, dude," he said.

"Don't you mean insects?" asked Ted.

"That's right," Evan agreed. "You catch on quick."

Then he got to his feet and clapped his hands to get the attention of the rest of the Backpackers.

"Okay, everybody. Let's work on our casting!"

What followed was *A River Runs Through It* filmed in an upside-down universe. Strange, not-very-good-looking people thrashed the air and water with wild swoops of fishing line. There were spectacular snarls involving three or more lines, swearing, and some crying. And that was just me and Wallace, Ted, and Renée.

Everybody else did fine. Even so, Evan appeared deeply stressed by lunchtime. He had to spend most of his time with us because we were so bad. After a few moments of watching us try to cast, he was covered in a thin sheen of sweat. By the end of the lesson he'd begun to flinch every time Wallace moved his arm. At one point Renée, in her enthusiasm and desire to please, cast as hard as she could to "really get it out there" and the entire rod went sailing into the lake. Evan cried, "Oh, shit!" with quite a bit of feeling. Keeping one hand over his head as if to ward off falling bombs, he rushed into the lake after it, muttering, "Don't cast, don't cast."

"Sorry," apologized Renée when he emerged. "Sometimes I don't know my own strength."

"Shot put. Fly fishing. Everybody gets them confused," he said, his lips slightly blue from hypothermia. Then he suggested that our group break early for lunch.

We chose a large flat rock to sit on and wait for the less spastic Backpackers to join us. As we unpacked our lunches it became clear that if we didn't catch a fish Renée might starve to death.

I took out my two made-by-Devlin muffins and a bottle of water from the *Owl* backpack. Wallace unloaded various store-bought items, and Ted unpacked a hearty and healthy balanced lunch. Renée stared hungrily at our food as she extracted a single carrot stick, a lonely radish, and a can of chocolate-flavored food substitute from a brown paper bag.

"Is that all you're going to eat?" I asked. "You're

working pretty hard out there, what with the rod throwing and everything."

"She's trying to go anorexic," reported Wallace.

"Laugh now, but when I'm the hottest girl in Junior Backpackers you won't be laughing."

"You're almost the hottest girl in Junior Backpackers now," said Wallace, at which point I decided he was a most excellent fourteen-year-old.

"Almost?" asked Ted.

"Shut up, Ted," said Wallace, and the nice moment was over.

After lunch we endured fly and hatch identification lessons. This involved staring at photocopies of bugs and then squatting by the lake to see if any of the little specks floating or buzzing around the surface matched. Then we stared at flies made out of bits of wool and feather and thread tied around a fishhook. At least, I think that's what the lessons involved.

The truth is that I was distracted because I was checking Evan out. I couldn't help it. I think he noticed, because he kept looking up and smiling at me and gave me extra attention. Jeanine noticed and shook her head in a gesture I couldn't quite interpret. She was probably just jealous.

I watched Evan take off his button-down shirt and crouch over the fly display in his T-shirt, talking to Ted. I found myself wishing it would get even hotter so he'd take off his T-shirt too. I was just thinking about what nice arms he had when Wallace interrupted me.

"Renée isn't feeling well. I think you better do something."

I went to find her sitting away from the group.

"You okay?"

"She's sick from not eating enough."

Renée didn't say anything. Her round face was pale against her radiant, explosive hair. But it was always pale unless we were hiking.

"Renée? Do you need some more food? I've got another muffin."

She shook her head.

"She's too pale," said Wallace. "You should be keeping an eye on her."

"Oh, Wallace," said Renée.

I gave her a muffin and she stared at it without enthusiasm before taking a bite.

"Good," I said. "You'll feel better soon."

"I told you I was fine."

Wallace made a snorting noise and then instructed

me that I'd better watch her carefully on the way down. "In case something happens."

When the lesson was over Wallace came with me to hand in our rods to Evan, who was loading up the truck.

Being a group leader and all, I felt it was my place to say something mature and professional. "Thanks. That was quite interesting."

Evan stopped what he was doing and stared at me.

"Thank *you*."

I nodded.

"Can we go now?" Wallace asked, pulling on my arm. "I'm in sort of a hurry."

"Check you later, hon," said Evan as Wallace and I walked away.

"Why were you staring at that . . . that illiterate . . . fishing and hiking . . . sunglassed . . . idiot?" Wallace demanded as soon as the four of us started down the path.

"What?!"

"Come on," he said. "We saw you!" he accused. "Didn't we, Renée?"

She looked at the ground. "Well . . ."

"I did not look at him," I protested.

"Didn't you tell us your boyfriend went to Scotland? That you were going to be single and focus on your screenwriting? And now you're flirting with that moron. It's disgusting."

"It was not! I was not!"

"It makes me sick," he continued. "He's such a cliché."

"Look, Wallace—" I stopped. How do you explain nice arms to a fourteen-year-old? Did I care about nice arms when I was fourteen? I couldn't remember.

And before I could think of the words he was gone, stomping ahead of us with speed I didn't know he possessed.

"Wallace is just mad because he has a crush on you," said Renée.

Ted nodded in agreement.

"But he's only fourteen."

"Yeah, fourteen. Not four," Renée said in her Wise-One voice.

"Damn."

"The younger men/older women thing may be genetic," she speculated.

Just my luck.

THE BALLAD OF MAUDE MACLEOD

Thursday, July 29

I was just about to start cleaning the house and planning MacGregor's party this afternoon when the phone rang. I picked it up on the first ring, thinking it might be Goose calling to tell me he'd changed his mind; he wasn't going to stay in Scotland for a year and then go to school in Montreal. That he's realized that those things were really pretentious and he'd prefer to stay near me. Or maybe it was Vince calling to say he'd made a mistake. Or George calling to apologize for being so unavailable.

But it wasn't any of those people. It was the most chipper girl alive.

"Hi!" The voice was shrill with enthusiasm. "Is this Alice?"

Before I could answer she broke in again.

"Great! Oh. My. God. I'm sooooo glad to finally get you on the phone! This is Ashley, and I'm our senior class organizer! Isn't it great? We are going to have

SO MUCH FUN! We are going to have the BEST GRAD EVER!"

I thought I'd escaped the attentions of the "grad" people. They are the people who spend their entire high-school careers longing for their final year when they get to call themselves "grads" and spend every free moment thinking about "grad." As a busy screen-writer and person with multiple part-time jobs and a family to take care of, the whole senior year thing is not really a priority. Anyway, I'm not sure "grad" is even a real word.

While the girl on the phone paused to take a breath, I tried to put a face to the name. Smithers Senior Secondary isn't that big. I must have had a class with her. The problem was that there are about fifteen Ashleys in Smithers Senior Secondary (although there are none in the Alternative School, which is telling).

"Sorry, Ashley who?"

"Ashley Philpotts. I'm calling because we're hav-ing a pre-grad party at the gravel pit beside the Four Fields on August sixth. It's the big kickoff for our senior year." She paused significantly. "And we want you to come."

Was this person actually inviting me to a party? No

one from my school, with the exception of Karen, who operates by a different set of rules than everyone else, has ever invited me out before. Why now?

Apparently being in Grade 12 makes all social distinctions fall away, and people like Ashley Philpotts become incredibly democratic, to the point where they start inviting people like me to parties. A mere two months ago, Ashley Philpotts (all the Ashleys, actually) looked at me like I was something wriggling in the flour bag.

Maybe this party is where my carefree good times summer will begin, but I doubt it.

"I'm not sure," I hedged.

"You just HAVE TO!" shrieked Ashley. "It's going to be SUCH A BLAST. It's going to be SO FUN. You'll JUST DIE. Our year is going to be the FUNNEST EVER!"

"Most fun," I corrected.

"Exactly!" enthused the Organizer from Hell, and then she warned, "I'm going to make sure you come. I will WEAR YOU DOWN!"

"I'm sure you will," I said.

Later

Mother's last letter piled even more responsibility on
my overburdened shoulders.

Dear Alice,

*This is going to be a short letter because things
are very busy here. We have decided to revolu-
tionize the whole system! We are going to
introduce recycling, composting, and community
gardening to the Vancouver Island Regional
Correctional Facility! Isn't that great?*

*Samantha, who has been doing so well since
she got rid of that boyfriend, had the idea. It
turns out she has an extensive background in
hydroponics and would be willing to show us
how to start a greenhouse.*

*Marguerite and I are completely behind her.
We have a meeting with the warden and a
representative from Corrections Canada later
today. Marguerite wanted to do a PowerPoint
presentation, but we said that we wanted our
presentation to be more human-centric and
organic. She was offended. It turns out that
before she became a Raging Granny,*

Marguerite was an MBA who worked for a plumbing supply company. Their products weren't even environmentally friendly! Needless to say, that's not something Marguerite shared with us. We are trying to overlook her corporate past, but it's hard. Now every time she speaks, all I can visualize is her in a power suit selling high-volume toilets. It's not fair, but she really has lost a lot of credibility.

Well, darling, ta for now. Keep your fingers crossed for us. Can't wait to see you next month.

In answer to your question, I do have a little stash of money hidden for Mac's birthday. It's hidden in one of my Tibetan prayer pillows. Please use it to get him a present! I'm devastated that I won't be there, but I will be with you in spirit. Oh, yes, and the recipe for sugarless birthday cake is in my Holy Holistic! cookbook.

All my love,
Your mother

Like I'm not already completely careworn and loaded down with various pressures. Now I have to figure out which Tibetan prayer pillow she's squirreled away her money in *and* make a health cake! And I can't even get MacGregor to help me because I've decided this party is going to be a surprise.

Later

Finn and Devlin came over tonight. Devlin made us a very nice vegetarian stew and baked a fresh loaf of bread. Finn brought along a package of deli meat, saying he's worried about his iron levels. You know, if it weren't for Finn's uncanny ability to attract nice guys, we might have starved to death by now. I think they are both concerned about my dad, which is why they keep coming over to cook and help out. He hasn't found a job or even had an interview lately and he's slipping deeper into depression. He doesn't even open his copy of *What Color Is Your Parachute?* anymore. He just packs it around like a little kid with a stuffed animal. It must be doubly hard for him to be unemployed when he sees how effortlessly successful I am in the employment area. I sympathize. I really do.

MacGregor left after dinner for his Summer Science Club meeting (a group that seems to consist only of him, Helen, and this boy named Peat, whose parents must be very insensitive to have named him after moss), and I told Finn, Devlin, and my dad about my plans.

"As you know, Mac's birthday is on Tuesday," I said.

Finn and Devlin turned around from where they were doing the dishes, and my dad looked up from where he was sweeping the floor.

"Dad, you're just pushing that dirt around," I said. Because I couldn't help but notice that his sweeping technique was nothing like the one Devlin showed us last week.

"Anyway, I'm planning this big surprise party for him."

"That's great," said Devlin.

"And let me guess," said Finn, who has a more suspicious nature. "You'd like us to help?"

"That's right," I said. "My idea is that I will *plan* the event. You know. Think up the plan. And then you will *execute* the plan. Does that sound good?"

Since I became a screenwriter with multiple jobs, I've gotten quite good at delegating. It's an essential skill in the film industry. But for some reason the delegatees balked.

"So your idea is that you think up work for us to do and we do it?" said Finn.

"That's a bit of an oversimplification."

"Sounds okay to me," said Devlin, who really is quite a pleasant person. But Finn interrupted.

"I think it might be better if you *thought of the plan* and then you *implemented the plan*. And if you have trouble, we can help out. By taking Mac to the movies. Or for pizza with his friends or something."

I squinted at him.

"What are you saying?"

"He's saying everyone is tired of you princessing around here, telling everyone what to do, never helping, and just thinking about yourself," said my father, whose resentment at my employment and artistic success is closer to the surface than I suspected.

"——!" I gasped, and gave them my I-can't-believe-this look.

My dad just went back to sweeping and Finn and Devlin turned back to the dishes.

"Fine then," I said bitterly to their backs. "I'll do it all myself. And you'll see. It's going to be the best party you've ever seen."

"Great," said my dad, without lifting his head.

Later

I'll show them. Mac's party is going to be the most incredible event ever held for a lower-income child by a sister who also lives below the poverty level.

OF MOOSE AND MEN

A SCREENPLAY BY ALICE MACLEOD

ACT II
SCENE 4:
FADE IN.
SMALL BUT ATTRACTIVELY
DECORATED HOUSE—DAY

GIRL stands in a small but nicely appointed living room. She is carrying a clipboard and has an air of quiet, attractive determination about her. She looks around her, sizing up the artistic possibilities of the small but handsome space. You can tell that she sees things that ordinary event-planners do not.

GIRL

(In a quiet, thoughtful murmur)
Hmmm. I think the band should
go here. And the surprise party
guests should stand here. And
the big surprise, the likes
of which have never been seen
before at a young boy's birthday party, will come in here!

*A figure enters at stage left.
It is the OTHER MAN! The one
who looks and sounds like Jamie
Oliver!*

OTHER MAN

Annette! I heard about your
effort to throw a party for
your disadvantaged brother
and how your wheelchair-bound
father and his alcoholic ne'er-
do-well friends refuse to help.
After all you've done for me, I
felt I had to stop by to offer
you my support! Please, tell

me, what is the theme of the party?

GIRL
(Humbly)
Thank you. But I must do this myself. I cannot accept your charity. And the theme of the party is Science.

OTHER MAN
I understand. Science. That is the most incredible party theme for a boy who likes science that I've ever heard of. And may I say how much I like your hair?

GIRL
(Touches hand hesitantly to head, which has been cut and is now excellent and ultramodern with an eighties flair.
She whispers.)
Thank you.

OTHER MAN

And because of all you've done
for me and my televised cooking show and the show where I
teach orphans how to cook, I'm
going to have my team donate
the cake.

*He waves his arm and in comes
an ORPHAN pushing a large
trolley cart. On it is a
cake shaped like the Hubble
Telescope!*

GIRL

Oh my goodness.
     *(Her voice is husky
      with emotion.)*
How can I ever thank you?

OTHER MAN

(Starts to speak.)
I—

*They are interrupted by the
entire cast of Cirque du
Soleil! The performers have
heard about the GIRL'S plight.
They all want to perform for
Annette, who is the next film-
making up-and-comer after
Quentin Tarantino and Sofia
Coppola! They come tumbling in.
Some of them do contortions.
Others sing. The clowns clown
around.*

OTHER MAN
*(Shaking his head in open
admiration)*
Leave it to Annette to get
Cirque for her disadvantaged
brother's birthday party.
*(He looks at her.
There is love in his eyes.)*

*They are surrounded by circus
performers. Beautiful musical
chaos ensues, similar to that*

> movie in which Nicole Kidman
> plays a dying prostitute and
> Ewan MacGregor is the writer
> who loves her and there is a
> lot of dancing.
> The GIRL and the OTHER MAN are
> lifted up by the performers and
> carried around.
>
> FADE OUT.

What a spectacle *Of Moose and Men* is going to be!

Friday, July 30

I must be a bit brain damaged from romantic disappointment! How could I forget that a couple of weeks ago Devlin gave Dad a Costco card as a sort of too-bad-you-are-poor gesture, which was quite nice of him. The birthday party is saved!

Dad wouldn't have dared take the card if Mom was home. She doesn't believe in shopping at big-box stores. She tries to "patronize small business." Patronize is right!

Mother is one of those shoppers who's blatant about the fact that she thinks she's doing local merchants a big favor when she buys anything. This is because she doesn't believe in commerce, capitalism, or money in general, really.

Embarrassing fact: My mother's been known to offer slightly damaged candles in exchange for cheese. Yes, it's true. She even tried bartering at the Grocery Giant once. I had the extreme misfortune to be there when my mom offered the checkout girl some of our Vanilla Serenity candles in exchange for a large piece of Gouda. Now *that* was embarrassing. I'll never forget the look on that girl's face.

Anyway, now we have a Costco card, my entrée to the biggest big box of them all. This may be the silver lining in my mother's incarceration. My not-very-large amount of money from my jobs is going to go a long way at a bulk food store. We are going to save the prayer pillow cash to buy Mac's gift. This party's going to be so good, I bet I'll be able to entice my brother to come home for the rest of the summer.

Later

Hints for new Costco members. Do not go without a list. Do not go without a set purchasing limit. And do not go with a person who has not had a decent meal since his wife went to jail.

I talked Dad into coming to Costco with me. We were nearly out of lentils, and I pointed out that Costco lentils probably cost half what they do at a normal store. The idea was that he would buy regular groceries while I picked up the birthday supplies. MacGregor was, as usual, at Helen's.

We went in at 1:00 and came out two hours later with $200 worth of stuff. Not just groceries, but stuff, including new fleece tops for the entire family ($15 each), 10-packs of sport socks ($10 each), and a barbell set ($25) for Dad's pectorals.

"Would you look at these!" exclaimed Dad, running his hands over the table piled high with fleece tops. "And the price!"

I was on the verge of telling him that we don't need fleece tops, but decided not to. After all, as a wilderness guide, I could probably use one.

Nor did I speak up when Dad came staggering back to the cart holding a package of muffins the size of a small futon.

"Look at these muffins!" he cried, struggling to keep the package in the air.

I considered pointing out the all-too-obvious pitfalls of forty massive bran muffins, not least of which was their lack of birthday party appeal, but held back again.

"What's that?" he asked, holding his back with both hands after wrestling the muffins into the cart.

"Nothing. They look good."

I have decided to serve fun food at MacGregor's party: veggie burgers, pasta. Stuff kids love. So we picked up an economy pack of 3,000 birthday candles, 1,200 yards of orange-and-black Halloween streamers (they were out of birthday colors), four pillow-sized bags of potato chips, and six giant bottles of no-name cola. We also bought a jar of mayonnaise that took up an entire cart by itself, a bag of pasta—which we are normally not allowed to eat due to the refined flour factor—weighing over twenty pounds, as well as a twelve-pack of relish for only $6!

For a special surprise we bought MacGregor a bag containing enough tropical fish food to feed every creature in the Vancouver Aquarium for a year.

We were set!

When we finally got to the till, Dad and I were each pushing our own orange Hummer-sized cart. I'd piled a bunch more fleece clothing on top of the mayonnaise jar. I didn't need any of it but it was so cheap I couldn't afford to leave it.

"I can't believe this place," exclaimed Dad. "This is the best time I've ever had!"

That was humiliating enough with just me as his audience, but a million times worse when someone who was not me answered him.

"Totally," came a voice. "There's nothing quite like having enough"—a glance into my dad's cart—"industrial-sized cans of mushroom soup."

I looked up, horrified, to see Evan smiling down at us from the Mount Olympus of good-lookingness.

"Hey," he said, smiling even wider.

"Hey. Hi. We're just, um, shopping."

"This must be your dad," he said, in a talking-to-parents voice.

"Dad, this is Evan. He runs the Junior Backpackers."

Dad was clearly impressed. "Oh, hey! Nice to meet you. We are really pleased that Alice has such a great summer job."

"Oh, we're totally happy to have her on board, sir," said Evan.

Sir! He called my dad "sir!"

Saying he didn't want to lose his place in the quarter-mile-long checkout line, Dad went on ahead.

"You must have a big family," commented Evan.

I made my face as blank as possible. Sometimes no answer is the best policy.

"So are you going to that thing next Friday?" he asked.

Thing? Surely he didn't mean the pre-grad party? Evan isn't in high school anymore. How would he know about the party?

"I don't know."

"You should. Your senior class just hired me to spin."

"Spin?" Why, oh, why am I so backward? I can barely speak English, I am so out of touch with the lingo of my generation.

"I'm DJ-ing. You know, spinning the tunes."

That was so cool I couldn't even respond.

"I like to see my staff having fun. Being social," he said. "You should go."

"Me?"

"No. That jar of mayonnaise you have there."

"Heh-heh," I said.

Then we were interrupted by a ruckus at the checkout.

"A hundred and ninety-two dollars!" came a

strangled voice. "But my daughter's still got another cart!"

Dad appeared beside my cart and, trying to be cool about it, whispered, "Do you have that money?" he asked, then added, "Also, I think we're going to leave some of that stuff for next time."

I handed the bulk fish flakes and my money to my dad. "Well, get these anyway. I'll put back the mayonnaise."

Evan walked with me as I drove the pig-sized jar of mayo back to the condiments aisle. It was like walking beside the sun. I couldn't even look directly at him, he was so radiant and overpowering.

He even looked cool maneuvering the jar back onto its shelf.

"So what do you think?" he asked.

"We don't need that much mayonnaise. It's probably okay that we didn't get it."

"I mean about the party."

For a second I was confused. Obviously, I was going to my brother's birthday party. Then I realized he meant the pre-grad party.

"Is my Number One Guide going?" he asked.

My stomach flopped, and I tried not to gulp.

"I don't know," I said. "I'm not really big on parties."

"I gotcha. But if you change your mind . . ." he replied.

As he walked away I had to steady myself so I didn't fall over. I may not be Number Four material but I was Evan's Number One Guide. Oh my god.

Saturday, July 31
The great thing about Costco muffins is that one pretty much does you for the whole day. MacGregor and I did a test this morning. We each ate one at 9:00 A.M. and we're waiting to see when we'll get hungry again. It's 7:15 P.M. and no signs of hunger yet!

I've made some very serious progress on the birthday party. I've called Finn and Devlin, and they've agreed to come. Karen can't attend because she's going out with her boyfriend, and Betty Lou has to do something else, so the party won't be that socially fun for me. But Karen did say she'd stop by before to help. Then I called Helen and got her to promise to call the rest of Mac's friends. Whew! I wasn't looking forward to tracking them down!

Other than that, I wasn't sure what to do. So I decided to call George. And for once she was available to talk.

We went through all the usual stuff, and I told her what I'd been up to: the birthday party, the jobs, the breakups. That took quite a while because I've been through a lot lately. When I finally finished I said, "So what's new with you?"

She was quiet for a minute. "Actually, there is something."

"You discovered the cure for hoof and mouth?" I said. "Ha-ha."

"Actually, I found out something else."

I waited.

"I've got some news, sort of."

Another pause.

She sighed. "It's like this. It turns out that, uh, Liv and I. We're really close."

"Yeah, I noticed."

"No. I mean, *really* close."

The full impact of what she was saying flooded over me. This was so after-school special! George, the most practical person on the planet, was having an issue and I got to respond. George! With an issue! Normally, I'm the one with all the issues. I had to handle this just right.

"Oh, yeah," I said, playing it nonchalant.

"That's it? That's your whole response?"

"I mean, sure. You're into girls now. That's cool."

"Girl. Not girls," she said. "Anyway aren't you surprised?" she asked.

I was a little, but I wasn't about to tell her that. I was going to be the understanding, open-minded friend, the after-school-special friend.

"Not really. Should I be? I mean, your name's George," I pointed out.

She exhaled in frustration. "Alice, that is just so, so . . . stupid. I can't believe you said that."

"What? I'm glad for you."

"Yeah, but you could be surprised at least. Instead of making assumptions."

"But I—"

"I think I've heard enough, Alice. Good-bye."

And then she hung up on me.

Okay. So I have no idea what I did wrong there. I'm *glad* George is gay now. That's the most exciting thing that I've heard all summer! She was a total pain when she dated that boy. She seems much happier now that she likes a girl.

Sure, I have a few questions. If George is a lesbian now, does that mean she was always a lesbian? And if so, did she ever have feelings for me? Because, I mean, I was right there, her best friend. And she never showed the slightest interest in me that way.

Which is kind of a concern, really. She showed irritation: yes. Interest: no. Maybe she just became a lesbian when she met Liv. My mom's given me all the books. I know sexuality is a continuum. Some people are very gay. Some people are a bit gay. And some people, such as myself, are apparently never going to have sex and don't appear on either end of the continuum. Damn, I wish he were still around. Goose and I could have had the best discussion about this.

Anyway, all creative people have a lot of gay friends. It's part of being an artist. If I could just get George to cooperate! I know, I'll call her back and pretend to be surprised. Like I was so surprised I didn't even realize it until later. But first I'll give her a chance to cool down.

This gives me an idea for a screenplay scene!

OF MOOSE AND MEN

A SCREENPLAY BY ALICE MACLEOD

ACT II
SCENE 5:
FADE IN.
ARTIST'S STUDIO—DAY

GIRL sits at large and fabu-
lous desk made of wood. The
implements of screenwriting are
arrayed around her. She has a
chipped tooth but a dynamic,
sporty fashion sense.
Knock at the door. Two GAY
GIRLS and two GAY BOYS come
in. They are the GIRL'S gay
friends. The girl is tremen-
dously popular in the gay com-
munity. She is almost an icon,
along the lines of Margaret
Cho, but not as funny.

GIRL
Hey, you guys!

GAY GIRL #1
(Who looks a bit like
Willow from Buffy)
Hey you, girlfriend!

GAY GIRL #2
(Who looks a bit like Tara,
Willow's girlfriend from Buffy)
I thought *I* was your girlfriend!

Everyone laughs.

GAY BOYS, who look a bit like
Will and Jack from Will and
Grace, start dancing. It's
shaping up to be a party in the
artistic GIRL'S writing studio!
Phone rings. GIRL, who looks a
bit like Grace, from Will and
Grace, picks it up.

GIRL
No, I'm sorry. I can't go out
with you tonight. I've got a
lot of friends over here.

We're having a terrific time.
  (She listens for a moment.)
That's right. My gay friends.
      (Listens again.)
I can't believe you just said
that. I'll tell you what. Why
don't you take your homophobic
bigotry back to the cave you
crawled out of? Don't ever call
me again.

(Hangs up the phone with a crash.)

GAY GUY #1

Annette, you are not only the
greatest writer I've ever
known, but you're also brave
and open-minded, with a totally
amazing fashion sense.

GAY GUY #2

I almost wish you were gay!

GAY GIRL #1

I know! Me too!

(Shoots a jealous look at GAY
   GIRL #1, thereby increasing
      the dramatic tension.)

Everyone dances to excellent
music that straight people don't
know about. And then everyone
takes turns enjoying GIRL's new
screenplay.

FADE OUT.

Now I just have to figure out where that scene goes in the whole scheme of the screenplay. Maybe it will be the beginning of a whole new screenplay. I wonder if I should share it with George.

Sunday, August 1
George called at 7:30 this morning. She is such a veterinary student sometimes.

But the great part is that she apologized! That's practically the first time she has apologized to me. It turns out I have George's new girlfriend to thank.

"Am I calling too early?" asked George.

"I was still sleeping, if that's what you mean."

"Too bad," she said. "Liv and I were talking. She said I might have been a bit hard on you."

I tried to wake up quickly so I could enjoy what I could feel coming.

"Liv says that I'm still getting used to the shift in my identity. She said I shouldn't be so touchy."

"I'd have to agree with her," I said, thinking of all the times George had torn a strip off me for some dumb thing I'd said.

"It's just that people are so stupid. Assuming that I'm gay just because my nickname is George and I don't wear makeup."

"But you *are* gay," I said. "At least you are now."

"I'm going out with a woman now. Only I get to decide whether I'm gay or not," she said.

Even though I was confused, I said, "Okay." And I decided that maybe I wouldn't share my screenplay with her just yet.

"This is a big deal to me," she said.

"Have you told your parents?"

"Yeah."

"And?"

"They tried to be all blasé. My mom was all, 'We *have* listened to k.d. lang, you know.' Like they're so progressive."

I didn't get this. "George, I know this is a big thing for you. And that it might be hard to get used to. But most people are still going to love you, gay or not gay. You're pretty great."

"Shut up," she said. But I could feel her smiling. Then she added, "That's what Liv says."

She wished Mac a happy birthday and told me she hoped his party worked out, and then we hung up and everything seemed okay. But now I find myself wishing I were gay and could get some much-needed acceptance and open-mindedness from the people around me. Also, George seems to be having a lot more luck in the relationship arena as a lesbian than I do as a straight person. Although she had more luck when she was a straight person too.

Later

Dear Goose,

I've written you about ten messages and deleted all of them. It seems like every time I get some news, I want to tell you about it. The latest is that George is a lesbian now. She's being very George about it. Her girlfriend sounds nice. At least nicer than that Barry guy she met at 4-H.

I wish you were here so we could gossip about this and make wild speculations. Or I could and you could tell me not to be such a gossip.

BTW: Have you done it with the Scandinavian yet? No! Don't tell me. I don't want to know.

Okay, I'm going to erase this now and go finish planning MacGregor's surprise party.

I miss you.

Love,
Alice

Monday, August 2

I may be an overworked party planner, but I still summoned up enough energy to spy on Bob's girl-friend for him.

When I broke away from my intensive work pre-paring for Mac's party tomorrow to go in and help Betty Lou today, I asked her probing questions such as, "So, are you getting any new tattoos?"

To which she replied, "I'm always getting new tattoos. Once you start you don't stop."

"Whereabouts?" I asked, half an hour later, so she wouldn't get suspicious.

"Wherever," she said, not really paying attention.

Aha! That explained why she had to remove black, lacy things.

"Kyle seems nice," I commented.

"He's okay," she said. "Hand me that stapler? This Kaffe Fassett poster keeps falling down."

Not much reaction there. No, she probably isn't having an affair with Kyle the Tattoo Guy. Bob is safe.

After I helped Betty Lou make more labels and put away yarn, she finally gave me a knitting lesson.

At the risk of sounding like Teen Talk Barbie on the subject of math, I discovered that knitting is hard. I was disappointed because, from what I hear knitting is the new yoga AND the new black. Any halfway plugged-in person wants to be able to do it. It goes without saying that a potential art knitter should be able to knit backward and forward, so to speak. But Betty Lou showed me about fourteen times, and I still kept screwing up.

I used a very radical and chic variegated yarn to practice. I told her I might make myself a dress, but she suggested I start with a scarf. After two hours I'd managed to make a *thing*, approximately two inches long, full of holes and studded with knots.

"How's the dress coming?" she asked, shades of bad old Betty Lou.

"It's a scarf now," I told her. Then I went out to get us each a veggie wrap from the little place on Main Street. We knitters need to keep up our strength.

When I came back I found Wallace on my stool, immersed in conversation with Betty Lou. They stopped talking as soon as I approached.

"Wallace, what are you doing here?" I asked.

He rolled his eyes and I noticed that with their eyeliner and black hair, he and Betty Lou could be sister and younger brother.

"We were just discussing, um, knitting," he said.

Betty Lou smiled down at her needles and yarn.

"Well, I gotta go," he said. "Very busy. No time for chitchat."

And as the door closed behind him, Betty Lou laughed and said, "Man, if I was fifteen years younger."

She's so weird.

Later

It turns out that it's not just knitting that's hard. *Baking* is practically impossible! I got Helen to invite MacGregor and poor Peat, the kid named after moss, to her house for a late-night Discovery Channel nature-athon, so I could cook for his surprise party tomorrow.

My dad was sticking to his guns in the not-helping department. Even when the icing caught on fire (in future all my icing is coming out of a can) and the cake fell and turned into a brown, granitelike slab, he didn't assist.

Then the salad turned into mush when I overcooked the pasta. All we get around here is brown rice, which takes about an hour to cook. How was I supposed to know pasta only takes ten minutes? So I was exhausted and frustrated and on my last legs, cookingwise, when Karen showed up and saved the day.

I can't believe how competent she is in almost every area. I was too distracted to answer the door because I was trying to stir the pasta to see if that would get it to harden up a bit, you know, the way that stirring porridge helps it to thicken. Apparently, the same principle does not apply to pasta.

"You have a visitor," said my dad. Then he gestured

around the kitchen and said, "As you can see, Karen, Alice is whipping up a little something for her brother's birthday party tomorrow."

Karen took in the still-smoking pot of icing, the evil little puck of brown cement cake, and the large glass bowl of off-white mush.

"I'm guessing your mom normally handles the birthday cooking," she said.

Too upset and frustrated to speak, I just nodded.

"I like baking." Karen stepped carefully into the kitchen. "Want some help?"

Another miserable nod.

And an hour and a half later, a beautiful cake containing actual white sugar and white flour sat cooling on the counter. Karen refused to make my mom's health cake, saying that we'd just end up with another petrified turd if we didn't put unhealthy ingredients in. She showed me how to make pasta and I really enjoyed throwing it at the wall, even though she said just tasting it was usually sufficient. She even explained the concept of putting a dent in it, so it's still firm. I couldn't quite follow that part.

While Karen was making the icing, the phone rang. It was Ashley, the Psychotically Enthusiastic Grad Organizer.

"Alice!" she screamed. "I told you I'd keep calling! I don't want you to forget the party."

"That would be the funnest ever party?" I asked.

She didn't correct my English. Instead she shrieked, "That's right! It's going to be so great! You're coming, right?"

"Um, well, I—" I wasn't really in the mood for a grad party, especially since I was just a charity guest.

"I'll call you twice a day until you say yes!"

"I've got a lot going on right now."

"Oh, that SUCKS!" shrieked Ashley. "I won't give up! Our year is going to be the BEST EVER! And I want EVERYONE to be a part of it."

"Yeah, well. Thanks," I said.

When I got off the phone I told Karen about Ashley's relentless invitations.

"Alice the iconoclast refuses to go to her own pre-grad party," she said, wiping off the counter. Somehow, while she was baking, Karen managed to get our kitchen cleaner than it has been since Mom went to jail. Karen must be the queen of Home Ec.

"So you're going?" I asked.

She gave me a look.

"Oh, that's right. They probably wouldn't even hold it without you."

Karen didn't argue. She really is very popular.

"You might like it. It's just Grade 12s," she pointed out. "You can come to my house to get ready."

I hesitated. That last time I went to party with Karen it didn't turn out well. She got drunk and left me to have a bottle of beer poured over my head by the toughest girl in town.

"I don't think so."

Karen shrugged. "Okay. But the invitation's open if you change your mind."

I can't think about it right now. I have my hands full with planning the birthday party, which I'm sensing is going to be fantastic.

OF MOOSE AND MEN

A SCREENPLAY BY ALICE MACLEOD

ACT II
SCENE 6:
FADE IN.
HOUSE—DAY

*A small but attractive house
has been beautifully decorated
for a science-themed birthday
party suitable for a YOUNG BOY.
There are pictures of newts and
insects and solar systems everywhere. A GIRL with a great
haircut and cool ironic outfit
walks in carrying a cake shaped
like the Hubble Telescope.*

GIRL
Happy birthday, Antoine.

BOY
I can't believe you did all
this by yourself. Ever since

you got the movie deal that
has turned you into the next
Quentin Tarantino you have
done nothing but help and support your family, even though
your second project, a knitting film, didn't work out.
And now you've given me a
cake shaped like the Hubble
Telescope!

OLDER MAN IN WHEELCHAIR
(With emotion)
Happy birthday, Antoine. I know
I said I'd get you a new fish
tank filter. But since falling while trying to make lentil loaf, I've been confined to
this chair. I'm sorry I wasn't
able to make you a lentil loaf
for your birthday.

BOY
(Shoots a grateful look
at his sister.)

That's okay, Papa. I know
you're doing your best since
Maman went to jail.

GIRL
Don't worry, Antoine. With my
money from Quentin Tarantino I
bought Maman a video camera so
she could tape you a birthday
message.

*GIRL turns on the TV and
presses Play.*

(ON TV)
HIPPIE WOMAN
*(She has obviously been made
over by a professional. Her
hair is coiffed and her outfit is not purple or tie-dyed.
She looks like a new woman. She
speaks into the camera.)*
My darlings. It is your Maman.
Annette, you are the kindest

girl. In spite of losing your
one true love and your Maman,
you have saved the family with
your screenwriting talent. Not
only that, but you have sent a
stylist into prison to help me
look more updated. I can never
thank you enough.

GIRL
(*Nods modestly, her excellent
hair perfectly arranged.*)
It's nothing. This is Antoine's
day. Let us celebrate.

BOY'S little science friends go
wild at GIRL'S generosity. No
one notices the look of sadness in kind GIRL'S eye, except
perhaps her GAY FRIENDS, who are
there to lend support to her
because she is a great favorite
in the gay community. No one
knows the trouble GIRL has seen

*or the sadness of lost love that
she must cope with each day.*

FADE OUT.

Tuesday, August 3
Everyone but me had a fantastic time at MacGregor's party. All I got was more evidence that I am not considered attractive.

While Mac was out this afternoon, I put the black-and-orange streamers all over the house, and wrapped the bag of fish food. Dad went out and spent the prayer pillow money on Mac's main present, a secondhand microscope. At 4:30 the guests started to arrive. I had no idea my little brother had so many friends! This town is practically bursting with serious-minded young people! They, combined with my dad's friends, Marcus, Kelly, Finn, and Devlin, made for a very full house. It was practically impossible to keep everyone quiet for the fifteen minutes between when Mac and Helen were supposed to show up and when they actually did.

I had to yell at everyone several times to get them to shut up. I even threatened to throw one kid out if he kept puffing so loudly on his inhaler because of his fear of enclosed dark spaces (I asked him to crouch in the area behind the couch). It was all worth it when Mac and Helen came through the door and I gave the code words: "Well, hello there, MacGregor!" and everyone burst out of their hiding spots and yelled "Surprise!" My brother looked totally impressed and thrilled. When I told him that I basically did everything to arrange the party, except for cooking and inviting the guests, he was really quite moved.

It turns out he was already celebrating because he just found out that he and Peat and Helen just won first prize in the First Annual Northern Interior Regional Summer Science Clubs Competition for their re-creation of an Amazonian river ecosystem in a twenty-gallon tank. Who knew!?

Everyone loved the cake, and nobody made a big deal out of it when Finn and Devlin quietly ordered a few pizzas because there was only enough pasta for six guests. (I guess I should have listened to Karen when she said I should use a bit more of the twenty-pound bag, but I assumed that it would puff up like rice. We really haven't had enough exposure to pasta in this family.)

Mom called at the scheduled time and wished Mac

a happy birthday and congratulated me on arranging the party. She sounded in a good mood even though she was missing her only son's birthday party. My mother really has the right temperament for revolution. Then, just as we were getting off the phone with Mom, a reporter/photographer from the local newspaper arrived at our house. Tuesday must be a slow news day in Smithers. Apparently, the editors heard about Mac's big science win and knew that Mom was in jail for her environmentalism and somehow they got this idea that we were this very notable and newsworthy family, sort of like the Suzukis.

The reporter, who is also the photographer, took pictures of Mac, Helen, and Peat with their trophy, and pictures of Dad, because he is very good-looking and married to my mother, the "eco-warrior." He took random party shots, a picture of Betty Lou because of the yarn store, a picture of Devlin because he's the new chiropractor in town, and more shots of Peat and Helen. He interviewed Finn about his used sporting-goods business and got a quote, which he called "priceless" because it was so witty. Then the photographer said he was so taken with Dad's "look" he asked him to model for an upcoming advertising insert. The only person he completely ignored was me! He didn't take any pictures of me! None. And I even wore two of my most innovative outfits.

Did I mention I was wearing a really cool outfit? First I had on my modified tennis/golf outfit of pleated skirt, argyle sweater vest, tam, and striped tube socks with tennis shoes. But my witty and ironic fashion statement seemed lost on the photographer, who just looked at me and Finn (who for some insane reason was wearing a white visor, a cravat, and a white T-shirt under a navy blazer, and almost unbelievably terrible white pants), and said, "Hey, are you two related?" I probably should have taken the time to tell him Finn and I are not related; that I am in fact a member of the very note- and photo-worthy MacLeod family. But I was so horrified, I instead rushed to my room and changed.

When I came out in my new thrift store riding outfit, the photographer was gone! I missed my shot at stardom!

I was so devastated I could hardly help with the post-party cleanup, a fact that my dad pointed out several times. How can he expect me to do manual labor when I'm this depressed? It's simply not reasonable.

Mac tried to reassure me that it didn't matter. He

pointed out that my picture appeared in the paper when I was a Miss Smithers candidate.

"It's not the same," I said. "They have to take the photo voluntarily for it to count."

He looked at me with sympathy and then went back to doing the dishes.

Wednesday, August 4

I just watched *Mask.* It's this excellent movie about a boy with a facial deformity who is very nice and smart and has a lot of challenges to overcome. The boy's feisty but unfortunately heroin-addicted mother is played by Cher. No one picks on the boy because his mom's very fierce and knows a lot of bikers.

It occurred to me that I am worse off than the boy in the movie for the following reasons:

1) My mom may not be a junkie, but she is in jail and doesn't even have any biker friends to protect me.

2) The boy manages to get a girlfriend when he lands a job as a counselor at a camp for the blind. But Smithers doesn't have any organizations for the blind. (Although in my case the clients wouldn't have to be completely blind, because I'm more homely than disfigured. Just really nearsighted would be fine.)

Also, let's face it, underneath the mask, the guy is actually Eric Stoltz, who is incredibly hot. There's no one under my mask but me.

Things are getting quite serious when I envy a person whose head accounts for half his body weight.

Later

Dad's been preening around all day, but in this very covert way. He doesn't want to get caught acting like a prima donna, but he totally is one. He's afraid to go out in case the photographer from the *Interior News*, or maybe someone from the Ford modeling agency, calls to offer him a modeling gig.

"Alice, I have to go out for a flash. Are you going to be around to catch the phone? Franz said he might call about our shoot."

"Franz? The newspaper guy's name is Franz? And you're going to let him take your picture?"

"What are you talking about? Franz is a perfectly good name for anyone, including a photographer."

"Anyway, since when do you go anywhere, especially for a flash?"

"Do I need to ask your brother? And when are you going to take down the streamers? I don't want them up this time next year. I thought we agreed that if you wanted to hold a party you would help clean up afterward."

"I'll get to it. It's just a few streamers. Anyway, I'm still caught on this flashing thing. Does Franz flash quite a bit?"

He gave me that look that good-looking people give not-so-good-looking people—you know, impatience—then asked MacGregor to take over phone monitoring. I went to write an e-mail.

Dear Goose,

I just put on the most amazing birthday party for MacGregor. I seem to have a lot of potential in the party-planning area. I mean, as long as I've got a large support team. Karen did the cooking and Finn and his boyfriend did everything else. But I am unbelievably good at hanging streamers. I think some of those streamers are going to be hanging for many years to come.

Did you ever find yourself thinking when we were together: "Gee, she's really not very attractive?" And if so, why did you overlook the fact? I was just wondering. This is just a hypothetical question because I'm going to erase this

*message, just like all the other ones I've written
to you.*

*Miss you. Hate your new Swedish girlfriend,
although I'm sure she's a very nice person.*

*Love,
Alice*

Oh, NO! I hit the SEND button! RETRACT!
DELETE!

Oh my god. It's gone.

Thursday, August 5

I think Ms. Deitrich just fired me from therapy.

I told her about the newspaper photographer and
how he wasn't interested in me because I'm not good-
looking enough and how I'm concerned that I may
not be a world-changer like my mother or attractive
like my father or brilliant like my brother. And I told
her how I accidentally sent my ex-boyfriend a pathetic
and insecure e-mail. I figured even a hard case like Ms.
Deitrich would be a bit sympathetic. But no.

She thought for a moment and then said, "I think
this is about choices."

I waited for her to elaborate.

She folded her hands on her desk in front of her.

"Let's examine. This photographer, who shoots your family and friends at the party. What is his topic?"

"I think he said it was going to be an article about local people who make a difference."

"So what have you done that's made a difference?"

"I help out around the house sometimes."

She frowned. "Don't be ridiculous. Something public, a business, a cause, a club of some kind."

"Nothing, at least not yet."

"Fine then. And how did you look at this party for your brother?"

"What do you mean?"

"You can't pretend you don't know that your sense for the fashion is unusual. This odd sporting wears. What is your intention with this? To be funny?"

I stared at her. This woman had all the sensitivity of a hammer.

"It shows I'm unique. An individual. It's about personal expression."

She didn't back down.

"The way you present yourself to the world is the lock to how you are received."

"You mean the key?"

She ignored me. "It's fine to be a different drummer. Just paddle with intention."

I exhaled a short, sharp, disappointed breath. Ms. Deitrich had really gone too far this time.

"I think that's very shallow," I said.

"That's reality," she answered. "There are kids in this Trouble Center with lives you cannot imagine. Or maybe you can. You do seem to have empathy as well as your self-centeredness. They have very real, very serious problems. And they cope. Most of them, anyway. It's time to stop the melodrama, Alice. You're a fine and perfect girl with health and a loving family. Maybe it's time for you to make some choices. You don't need a counselor to do that."

Session over.

Later

How dare she suggest that I'm fine and that I cause my own problems? At a minimum, I'm deeply misunderstood. Bob totally recognized that I have problems. In fact, his whole career is based on my issues.

I was so mad at Ms. Deitrich that when I got to the video store after our session I picked out all the stupidest, most mainstream movies I could find, even though I'm usually a fan of cutting-edge independent films. The first one I watched was *Pretty Woman* in which Julia Roberts plays a prostitute who gets picked up by a rich man and he makes her into a proper lady by getting her some new clothes. At first, when she still looks like a hooker, some shop ladies are mean to her. They get taught a lesson when she buys a lot of stuff from other stores and they don't get the commission.

The movie's a powerful message to people working in customer service to be nice to people who look like sex-trade workers because they might have money. It's also a powerful lesson about how if you want a nice life, you need really nice clothes because, just as I suspected, your whole life is determined by your clothes.

I liked the movie, even though it was dumb and Hollywood. Between it and Ms. Deitrich I'm starting to recognize that at least some of my problems may not be caused by me. They may be caused by my clothes.

I considered my riding outfit, which I've been wearing more or less constantly since the party. My jodhpurs have these big air pockets on the sides, probably in case my thighs develop huge riding muscles. I considered my slightly-too-small black jacket and tall rubber boots and then an image of Karen popped into my mind, immaculate in her capris and white shirt. Something clicked. I picked up the phone.

"Hi, Karen," I said. "I was just thinking. Remember what you said when you were helping me get ready for Mac's party?"

"You mean about taking pasta out when it's still slightly undercooked?"

"No. About our class party. You said I could get ready at your house."

She understood instantly. "We'll get ready at my house. And you can borrow some of my clothes."

"Seriously?"

"Sure. We can even give you a whole makeover if you want."

"Like Julia Roberts in *Pretty Woman*?"

"Well, it won't be quite so 'Bambi Meets Streetwalker,' but it's the same basic concept."

Although offensive to my ideals, the idea was sort of exciting. Karen could make me look nice! I could find out what it was like to be well-dressed. Then people would think I was traditionally attractive and I wouldn't get left out of photographs and dropped by my boyfriends.

"Are you serious?"

"Completely. This will be interesting," she said, sounding like a cook challenged to create an edible dish using strange ingredients, like one eggplant, two eggs, a bunch of beet tops, and three potato chips. I felt a flicker of hope. But it was very faint.

Still no message from Goose. Maybe he's changed his e-mail address. Or blocked mine. I can only hope!

OF MOOSE AND MEN
A SCREENPLAY BY ALICE MACLEOD

ACT III
SCENE 1:
FADE IN.
ARTIST'S STUDIO—DAY

Unusual-looking GIRL sits at the large desk. Her GAY FRIENDS have gone off to be couples together. In fact, everyone is off being couples together, even Quentin Tarantino and the OTHER WOMAN who stole the GIRL's part

in the knitting film. The MAN
and the OTHER MAN are nowhere
in sight. They are probably off
with other, less unusual-looking
women. Although the implements
of screenwriting are arrayed
- around the GIRL, she is not
writing. One gets the sense she
hasn't written in a while. She's
cradling her head in her hands.
She looks like that statue,
Ruben's Thinker.
Nothing happens. The scene
stretches out in a terrible
silence. Finally the GIRL lifts
her head.

                    GIRL
             (Speaking quietly
              in the silence)
Okay. I'll do it. I'll give it
a try.
Ominous classical music plays
in the background. It's a sus-
penseful, sad, and frightening

```
moment. It's also hard to tell
what's going on.


FADE OUT.
```

Friday, August 6
I've never gotten ready at a friend's house before.
It was odd but also fun. Karen's room was very
unusual.

Everything was white. She'd covered the windows
with plain white muslin curtains and hundreds of
white paper airplanes hung from her ceiling. An
aromatherapy burner steamed away on her bedside
table, surrounded by tiny bottles of essential oils. The
paper airplanes rustled overhead when we moved,
producing an interesting effect in combination with
the heavy herbal fragrance and the damp heat.

I knew Karen had a lot of clothes, but I was still
surprised as she rustled through endless closets and
chests, opening and closing doors, running her hands
over racks and rows and stacks of clothes.

"Hmmm," she said, looking from me to the clothes.

I sat on her bed, feeling homely but also sort
of excited. My inner Julia Roberts was about to
be revealed!

I just wished Goose and Vince and Trent from the Number Four and that photographer from the *Interior News* were here to see the transformation.

"Now what we want is something that says you are detached, superior, but also approachable," mused Karen, lifting the tops of boxes of shoes and pulling out a series of matching tote bags, unzipping them, giving the contents a poke, and then zipping them again.

She turned to me and stared for a few more seconds, hands on her hips. Then she reached into a dresser drawer and, without looking, pulled out an article of clothing. She reached up to a shelf in her closet and grabbed something else. She paused at the shoes, a pair of blue flip-flops decorated with plastic flowers, to make sure she had the right ones in her hand. She held them up briefly and then switched the blue pair for a purple pair.

"Too many flip-flops," she murmured to herself. "A person can never have too many flip-flops."

She didn't ask me if I liked what she'd chosen. She just started changing the aromatherapy blend in the burner, blowing out the tea light and wiping out the bowl with a piece of paper towel, then rubbing it clean with a few drops of rubbing alcohol.

"Go ahead," she said, running her hand over her collection of little bottles. "Get dressed."

I was sort of embarrassed so I changed as quickly as I could. The white skirt she'd pulled out was short and stretchy and lined with some kind of silky stuff, and the tank top matched. Both of them were much smaller and tighter than my usual clothes. I held up the sheer T-shirt, wondering what to do with it.

"That goes over the tank," she said.

It was like wearing air, the slight tug of the fabric like a breeze on my skin.

"Shoes," she commanded, and I slipped on the flip-flops.

"Very nice," she said, looking me up and down.

I felt exposed, like I'd woken up from a dream to find myself standing in the middle of the forest, dressed in panties and a bra.

"Check it out," she urged.

I turned to the mirror in the corner. I almost couldn't look. There was something so obvious about the clothes. I felt like I'd disappeared and just left my body behind for people to look at.

I turned slightly and, feeling a bit shy, checked out the back view. It was like looking at someone else. Someone who wore tight clothes, someone who wanted to be sure that everyone knew she was a girl.

"But it's so white," I said.

"Sexy outfits frequently are," she said seriously. "You're into movies. What color was Sharon Stone wearing when she uncrossed her legs in that movie?"

"White."

"That's right. And what about the skirt Marilyn Monroe wore when she stood on that vent and her skirt blew up around her ears?"

"White."

"That's right."

"But I'm not planning on showing anyone my, you know, underwear. Or anything else."

Karen lounged on her bed. "You look hot," she said, as though it was a statement of fact.

I checked my reflection in the mirror again, and I had to agree. She was right. I didn't look like myself, but I did look hot.

"Just wait till I get finished with your hair and makeup," she said, looking supremely confident.

After we drove up the rough road, Karen turned into the opening to the gravel pit on the edge of the Four Fields. She parked off to the side, as far away from the other cars as she could get.

A large bonfire burned in the middle of the pit and the blaze was surrounded by vehicles parked end to end in a circle.

The scene was strange in the still light of the evening, like we'd just stumbled on people searching for aliens in the Arizona desert. At least, that's how it felt until Ashley the Organizer spotted us.

She screamed and came running over.

"Oh my god! Alice? Is that you? You look so fantastic!" Then she peered in to look at my chipped tooth. "Except for your tooth. But still, looking good, girl." She pretended to get a burn on her finger from touching me. "Tssss!"

Then she turned to Karen. "Omigod! Karen! It so wouldn't be a party without Karen Field! We are going to have such a blast. This is going to be the best grad class ever!"

Ashley reminded me of one of those mechanical toys that buzzes along the ground bumping against things until someone sets it going in another direction. She was relentless.

"Come on!" She grabbed our hands and pulled us after her.

It was like every single person at the party had been lobotomized and turned into this enthusiastic, happy thing called a "grad." These weren't alien researchers. These were actual aliens.

People who had not spoken a word to me since I returned to regular school a year ago came up and hugged me. People who'd actively made fun of the fact that I took most of my classes at the Alternative School screamed into my face that they were SO GLAD I CAME. And because I was wearing a tight, white outfit and had sleek, manageable hair and flawless makeup, I seemed to have no defenses. No irony, no sarcasm. It's very hard to be detached when your entire body is hanging out there for everyone to see.

Soon Karen and I were leaned up against somebody's truck with bottles of something sweet and alcoholic in our hands. I looked over nervously to see how Karen was doing and was relieved to see her put her drink on the bumper.

I caught a glimpse of Evan. His turntables and equipment were set up in the back of a truck on the far side of the pit. He wore big headphones, and when I looked in his direction I saw him staring over at me and his big white teeth flashed a smile. Suddenly, I felt even more exposed.

I couldn't focus on the sudden flush of anxiety because I was surrounded by a swirl of soon-to-be

Grade 12s, almost all of whom seemed if not drunk, then pretty much out of their minds with excitement. They all wanted to tell me how much they used to hate me and reassure me that they didn't anymore because "it's like we're all graduating together." Some of them wanted to apologize for "being so shitty" to me and all of the other people who go to the Alternative School. Ashley and her friend "Bren" explained why they invited me.

"Last year's class didn't even invite the people from the Alternative to their parties. I'm not even sure they were invited to the ceremony. Hey, Bren, isn't that right?"

"Huh?" Bren replied, interrupted while staring at her nails.

"Yeah, so we're really trying to be more, like, democratic and inclusive and everything."

Constrained by my tight white outfit and shiny pink lipstick, I couldn't even give that the response it deserved. Instead, I just nodded when she screamed our class chant in my ear: "We Rock. We Rule. All before were just tools." Or maybe it was "Anyone else can just drool." I couldn't quite tell.

Again, the outfit prevented me from reacting.

After they finished confessing how much of

a loser they'd always thought I was before we all became Grade 12s, the girls morphed into my Very Best Friends, linking arms with me and dragging me around to talk with all the other girls who'd also "always thought I was totally weird" but now couldn't wait to hang out with me because we were all part of the "best graduating class ever."

A person wearing a Sex Pistols T-shirt, striped leggings, and a kilt would have had some defenses against crap like that. But a person wearing sexy white clothes has to take what she can get. So before long I found myself dancing (that's right—dancing!) with about six other girls while Karen stood surrounded by overawed boys and her usual posse of shiny, popular friends.

Surreal doesn't even begin to cover it.

While we were dancing, I looked over a few times to see Evan staring at me. Lightheaded from the diabetic-coma-inducing sweetness of two coolers, I had to close my eyes for a few minutes to be sure I wasn't imagining things.

As darkness dropped softly into the gravel pit the party sped up and, beyond the edge of the firelight, slowed down. People who weren't Grade 12s, older people, started to arrive and the crowd became denser. Arm in arm with the other frenzied people from my class, I rushed from group to group, now dancing with the Ashleys, now talking to the people smoking pot in the Volkswagen van. I saw Karen chatting with the official grad graffiti painter, the boy whose job it would be to paint the name of our class on rocks and underpasses around town. Then I turned to find Evan standing right behind me.

He didn't say anything over the pounding music but crooked his finger to indicate that I should follow him.

By now I felt not just a little drunk, but also a little overheated, like the bonfire had singed my lungs and my skin. I didn't cool off at all as I found myself facing Evan, the world's most attractive outdoorsman, at the dark outer edge of the party.

"So you came," he said.

I could smell the beer on his breath.

"Are you having fun?" he asked. "Because I want my Number One Guide to have fun."

I nodded dumbly.

"You look really good," he said. "Even the first time I saw you, when you were wearing that fucked-up outfit, I said to myself, 'That's nice.'"

I just barely stopped myself from gaping at him and saying shut up. Evan just said I was nice. No. Not nice. He said I *looked* nice.

I tried not to fall over. I was painfully aware of my moth outfit glowing softly in the moonlight.

"Ha-ha," I said, my head spinning. My boss, the most beautiful man in Smithers, just referred to me as though I were an inanimate object. But it was a compliment. I felt thrilled and a little sick that he had just called me a "*that.*"

"You want to go sit in my truck? It's right over there."

Some small fear tugged at me and I said, "No. I mean, no thanks."

"Well, let's just sit over here, then."

I found myself perched precariously on a fallen tree, with Evan's arm around me. Goose's face and then Vince's came into my mind, but my head kept whirling and next thing I knew I was kissing Evan, my boss, and it was like I'd just dropped a rope I'd been using to climb a mountain and I was falling. My nose was full of his smell and he tasted like salt beneath the yeasty sweetness of the beer.

Then, as so often happens when I end up in a kissing-type situation, we were interrupted.

I heard a loud rustle and a ghostly face with black depressions where the eyes should be loomed out of the darkness.

The face made a small coughing sound.

I pushed Evan back and tried to focus.

"What the hell?" asked Evan.

The face came closer.

"Dude!" said Evan, startled at the face's other-worldly aspect.

"Hey, Evan. I was just wondering if I could talk to Alice."

If I looked hard I could just barely see the outline of the body the face was attached to.

"Wallace?" I asked.

"Yes?" came the voice.

"What are you doing here?"

Wallace's disembodied head gave another small cough.

"We heard there was a party."

"Wallace, man. What are you doing?" said Evan, taking his arm off my shoulder.

"We just need to talk to Alice."

"We?" I asked. "Who's we?"

Somewhere in the inky blackness Renée's voice piped up.

"Hi."

"Is that you, Renée? You guys totally shouldn't be here," said Evan. "I might have to speak to your parents," he said, but I noticed he had moved a bit farther away from me.

"Yeah, I'm sure. Anyway, we just want to talk to Alice for a second," said Wallace.

"I'm right here."

"Yeah, so we were wondering if you could give us a ride home."

"You came all the way out here to ask me for a ride home?"

"Whatever," said Evan, getting up. "I've got to get back."

"Good," said Wallace.

That was the end of my first Grade 12 party. I went to get Karen, and she drove me and my two Junior Stalkers home. I tried a few times to get Wallace or Renée to tell me how they ended up at the Four Fields but they weren't talking.

All was quiet until Wallace spoke up from the backseat.

"I hate your outfit. It doesn't suit you at all," he said.

Renée disagreed. "I think it's awesome."

"Thanks," replied Karen.

We dropped Wallace off first. He lived out past the airport in an enormous house made of logs and surrounded by fenced paddocks.

"Big house," I commented.

Wallace got out and walked around to my side of the car. "This could all be yours someday," he said and then stood to the side and watched us turn around and pull away.

"Intense kid," said Karen.

"You have no idea," said Renée.

Saturday, August 7

I could make a big deal of the fact that I was kissed by a grown man who is also incredibly, painfully attractive. I could also spend my time worrying that a fourteen-year-old goth is stalking me. Luckily, as an artist/screenwriter, I'm focused on the here and now. So I think I'll do a bit of writing while I'm waiting for Evan to call. I'll probably finish *Of Moose and Men* very soon. Now that I no longer need therapy, I've got a bit more time on my hands.

OF MOOSE AND MEN

A SCREENPLAY BY ALICE MACLEOD

ACT III
SCENE 2:
FADE IN.
INSIDE OF CAR PARKED ON
STREET—DAY

GIRL sits inside car. She is
extraordinarily attractive
and well-dressed in clothes
she's made herself. Sort of
like Pretty in Pink only more
attractive and not as pink. She
has a tiny but undeniably sexy
chip out of her tooth, probably
made while applying very expen-
sive lipstick.
There is a knock at the car
window. A very attractive OUT-
DOORSMAN stands outside. He has
a fishing rod in his hand. He
is very, very attractive and is
wearing hiking boots.

GIRL
(Rolls down window.)

OUTDOORSMAN
Hi.

GIRL
(Shy about chipped tooth,
which is quite sexy,
puts hand over her mouth.)
Hi.

OUTDOORSMAN
I've been wanting to talk to
you for a long time. I just
really think you're attractive.
Oh yeah, and smart.

GIRL
(Smiles. Hand slips, revealing
sexy chipped tooth.)

OUTDOORSMAN
Would you like to go out with me?
I mean, before I have to go back

to work on my nationally syndi-
cated fishing and hiking show.

GIRL
(Very femininely)
Okay.

We see OUTDOORSMAN walking away.

OUTDOORSMAN
(Speaking to himself)
That's the most incredible
woman I've ever seen. And I've
seen a lot. She's beautiful,
worldly, and the best natural
fly caster I've ever seen.

FADE OUT.

Hmmm, I'm not sure how this fits with the scene
before. Oh well, the best films often don't make
any sense. I'm a little surprised that I've had time
to finish an entire scene, and Evan still hasn't called.
That's odd. Maybe I'll just write another scene, while
I'm waiting.

SCENE 3:

*A fairly attractive and stylish
GIRL in her room. Phone is
ringing. GIRL picks it up.*

GIRL

Oh hi, Ben. No, I'm sorry. I
can't go out with you tonight.
I've got that awards ceremony
to go to.
   (Hangs up. Phone rings again.)
Larry! Thanks, yeah. I know.
My agent says it's going to be
huge. This afternoon? No, I'm
sorry. I just can't do it. I've
got that thing.
         (Phone rings again.)
Janeane Garofalo? Of course
I know who you are! You are
so smart and funny. Are you
serious? I'm the main inspi-

ration for your work? Well,
that's amazing. Sure, I'll go
to the MTV Music Awards and be
a presenter. For you Janeane,
anything!

(Gets off the phone and lies
back on her bed.)

Ever since I wrote the screenplay for that hit movie I've
been so busy. It's been really
hard for people to get through
to me on the phone.

FADE OUT.

Evan still hasn't called. I hope he's not on that annoying three-day plan too. I'll just write one more scene
and call it a night.

12:15 A.M.

SCENE 4:
Somewhat attractive GIRL lying
on bed. Phone rings. It's

Janeane Garofalo. *She leaves*
a message about the MTV Music
Awards. But GIRL doesn't move.
This goes on for quite some
time. Suddenly, tall OUTDOORS-
MAN breaks down door and comes
crashing into room.

OUTDOORSMAN

Annette? Annette? Are you all
right?

OUTDOORSMAN shakes GIRL. She
doesn't move. In fact, she
appears lifeless.

OUTDOORSMAN

Annette! Please wake up!

GIRL doesn't wake up.

OUTDOORSMAN

(Heart-rending tone in voice)
No! Please. Don't be dead of a
rare heart condition because

I was late getting you your
medication. I'm sorry I was
late! I'm sorry. My life is
destroyed. My fishing and hiking show will get canceled and
I'll never know love again.
     (OUTDOORSMAN throws himself
         over girl and gives heart-
              rending cry.)
Nooooooooo!

FADE OUT TO THE HAUNTING AND
SENSELESS SOUNDS OF ONE OF
WAGNER'S MORE FRIGHTENING OPERAS.

I may have lost control of the plot of *Of Moose and Men*, but I'm sure that's something the director can fix.

Evan must be on the three-day plan. He still hasn't called but someone else has called twice and hung up. I suspect it's Wallace. I'm going to have a talk with that boy.

Sunday, August 8

Too depressed and anxious to write much. I hate the three-day plan. I wish I were still in therapy. I hate being responsible for my own life.

At least Goose isn't on the three-day plan. It's been four days since I sent him that message by accident, and he hasn't replied.

Why is romance so horribly confusing? No matter how many makeovers I get, it always ends up with me waiting by the phone. I wish I didn't care. My mother might be able to explain it to me, but she's in jail and I'm just too depressed to write to her. I suspect she's not going to like Evan. She wouldn't understand how sexy it is to be talked about like an inanimate object by a handsome man.

Monday, August 9

I never thought I'd be relieved to go to work but for the second time I was happy to go help Betty Lou. I even showed up early for my shift. The yarn store is opening soon. I was looking forward to a few hours of shelving and labeling, followed by several hours of knitting and talking about important subjects, such as tattoos, knitting, and boys.

Even though I was early, Wallace beat me there. I

came in to find him huddled in deep conversation with Betty Lou. They both looked up when the doorbell chimed, and Wallace jumped off his stool.

He looked at me, his eyes huge and black in his white face. He didn't smile or say hello.

"Don't forget your yarn," said Betty Lou, and shoved a couple balls of black yarn and some needles toward him.

"Thanks," he said, and slipped them into the big pocket of his black trench coat. "Wouldn't want to get caught without my knitting."

He pointed to a CD on the counter and said to me, "For you." Then he swept out the door with his coat flapping.

"This I have to hear," said Betty Lou, as I opened up the case to check out the handwritten song list.

Betty Lou and I listened to Wallace's CD compilation that he'd labeled "Love Will Tear Us Apart," which was also the name of the first song.

When it came on Betty Lou said, "Oh my god. He put Joy Division on there. I'm not kidding, if I was just ten years younger."

When "I Hate Myself for Loving You" by Joan Jett came on, she looked at me and shook her head in wonder.

When "Friday I'm in Love" by the Cure started she put her hand over her heart and sighed. "I have to copy this."

That mix was so excellent I barely noticed when Betty Lou said she had to go next door for a minute. And when "What Are You Going to Do with Your Life?" by Echo and the Bunnymen began, I stood frozen in the middle of the store, paralyzed by the song's beauty. I didn't hear the door open. When I turned, somehow I wasn't surprised to find Vince standing just inside the door.

He stepped farther into the shop and cocked his head, listening.

> *If I could see what you can see*
> *The sun still shining out of me*
> *I'd be the boy I used to be*
> *When love was blind.*

When the song was over and I turned down the stereo, he shook his head.

"Quite a song," he said, and looked around. "So this is what a knitting store looks like."

Taking note of my tennis ensemble, including short, pleated skirt and visor, probably the most normal of my sports fusion ensembles, he said, "You forgot your racquet."

"You can do better than that."

"That depends on what you're wearing."

"True." I thought for a moment. "How did you know I was here?"

"Called your house."

"Oh."

"Yeah, so I just wanted to say hello. See how you're doing."

"Even though I'm so young and everything?"

He gave a small laugh. Then he leaned forward like he was going to kiss me. Instead, he reached out and moved a piece of hair from my visor's brim.

"See you later, Martina."

I watched him walk out the door in his kitchen whites, and nothing made sense to me at all.

Half an hour later I realized that Betty Lou still wasn't back, and I was ready to cast off. My *thing* was about fourteen inches long, six inches wide at one end and three inches wide at the other. I decided to go next door to ask Betty Lou for some help.

I walked through the door between the shops. At first, the inside of the Eternal Anchor reminded me of a hair salon. There weren't any customers, but there was a reception desk and leather sofas and a coffee table covered in magazines and books off to the side. I stared at the posters of Japanese girls with big colorful tattoos.

I didn't see Betty Lou or Kyle, so I headed to the back of the shop.

Four doorways, each hung with a black velvet curtain, opened off the short hallway. Three of the curtains were open and I could see a black leather-topped chrome stool and table inside each of the cubicles.

The curtain across the fourth room was closed partway. I looked in at a jumble of skin and black clothes and at first I wasn't sure what I was seeing. In my horror and shock, I dropped my knitting. Kyle turned as I stood there with my mouth hanging open and he said, a bit peculiarly I thought, given the circumstances, "Check it out."

I shut my mouth and tried to focus.

Betty Lou turned to me. She had a towel pressed to her front.

"Hey," she said.

I calmed down enough to see that Kyle sat on a high stool. He was wearing pants. And a shirt. He was dressed! Thank god. Betty Lou had her bare back to him. She was sort of leaning over a leather backrest. Her pants were on too. Whew! It was a pretty racy scene, but not what I thought.

I picked up my knitting and tried to avert my eyes. For some reason I felt even more embarrassed now.

"Have a look," Kyle urged me again. He seemed to find my discomfort amusing.

Keeping my eyes trained on the spot where the wall met the linoleum in the corner, I walked a little way into the room.

Like an artist working on a canvas, Kyle wiped Betty Lou's back. And there it was: Bob's face staring up from Betty Lou's right shoulder blade.

"What do you think?" she asked.

I stared and all of a sudden felt like crying.

"He has no idea. We've got to get this finished, so when I unveil it for him, he's not just looking at a bandage."

I nodded, my eyes full.

"You okay, Alice?" she asked.

I couldn't speak, so I just nodded once more and left.

It occurred to me as I was walking home that now I was a working woman. As a result, I tend to take things quite seriously and am careful and thoughtful. I have seen and done a lot, including receiving the best mixed CD ever made, basically graduating from therapy, and having a make-out session with the best-looking man in town. And in terms of domestic responsibility, I'm sort of like one of those men in the 1950s who went to work every day to support his family and was happy to do it.

Unfortunately, my dad is like one of those flighty 1950s females who is disobedient and ungrateful and has no idea that it's her part of the social contract to cook the meals and clean the house.

I said as much when I got home to find the house in disarray, and my dad with his towel-covered head over a steaming pot on the kitchen table.

"Hello, I'm home."

I looked around. No sign of food for the breadwinner.

"Just off work. Sort of hungry," I added, hinting broadly.

One of Dad's arms came up and pointed in the direction of the fridge.

MacGregor and Helen were in the living room mounting drawings of insects that they'd done for the upcoming Junior Naturalist exhibit.

"Why is Dad's head in a pot?"

"He's steaming his pores."

My brother is so evolved that he didn't even seem embarrassed by this fact.

"My mom makes me do that when I've got a cold," commented Helen.

"It's for his complexion," MacGregor added.

"I hope he fed you at least."

"I ate at Helen's. Dad had to go to the tanning machine this afternoon."

No wonder those 1950s men often died early due to excess stress.

Evan still hasn't called.

Tuesday, August 10

Still no phone call from Evan. Betty Lou didn't mention a four- or five-day plan. No phone call from Vince. No phone call from George. No e-mail from Goose. If it wasn't for my mixed CD I'd be pretty down right now.

Oh, well, on a happier note, MacGregor's been home practically constantly since the party.

Later

They say youth is wasted on the young. Well, it's not wasted on me. Not anymore.

To be honest, I'm not even sure *what* happened to me tonight.

Evan finally called.

"Hey. It's Evan."

The wait had turned my nervous anticipation into straight nervousness.

"Hi." I was afraid to say more in case he could hear my heart pounding through the receiver. I thought I might be hyperventilating.

"I'm at the Number Four. Why don't you come down here and meet us and come back to my place for a party later."

I struggled for breath and an answer.

"Um (huge, gasping intake of air), I (wheeze), don't (choke), know. . . ."

"Come on, hon," he said. "Wear that white dress."

What was I, an idiot? Obviously I wasn't going to go rushing down to my least favorite place wearing clothes that weren't mine and that didn't even reflect my true personality. That was a one-time-only experiment. Then I thought of Bob's face on Betty Lou's back and George and Liv and the next thing I knew I was back in Karen's tight white moth outfit, which, fortunately, I'd worn home after the party. Less fortunately, I hadn't had a chance to wash it yet, so it wasn't very clean. I tried to get the marks out with a wet cloth but every spot I rubbed ended up not only dirty, but also saggy. To compensate I wore more lipstick. I was glad my dad was on the computer with MacGregor, who was showing him how to find out more about career opportunities for older male models.

"I'm going out for a while!" I said, rushing past the doorway.

"Okay!" said my jovial, somewhat employed father.

And that was it. No "when will you be home?" No "who are you going to see?"

Scurrying along the sidewalk on my way to the Number Four, wishing I was invisible, I suddenly thought of Vince. I couldn't let Vince see me with Evan! Vince may have rejected me due to not wanting to be a perved-out older man with younger woman. But that didn't mean I wanted him to see me with a *different* older man.

I found myself standing outside the Number Four, stuck to the sidewalk, afraid to go in and afraid to go home.

Then I got the idea I could wave down one of the servers and find out if Vince was working or not.

I sidled up a bit closer to the window and peered

in. I could see the back of Evan's head in one of the booths. He was sitting with someone. The restaurant looked different somehow, darker.

Then I saw Geena. She was at Evan's table. I could see her laughing as he said something. I waited until she came my way and then I knocked softly on the window.

She didn't notice, so I knocked again.

This time the customer in the booth closest to the window leaned around. I smiled at his puzzled face and pointed at Geena.

He gave me a look that wasn't exactly filled with admiration, but he got her attention.

I made a frantic beckoning gesture and ducked out of sight again, my heart beating like crazy.

What the hell was I doing? This kind of stuff would be bad enough if I were wearing a long trench coat, but trying to sleuth around in a tight, white, dirty outfit was too much.

It seemed like hours before Geena made it outside.

"What are you doing out here?" she asked peevishly.

"Is Vince working?"

"No. Why?"

That called for some fast thinking. This not very smart girl would be seeing Vince again. She was sure to mention that I'd been lurking outside the restaurant asking about him.

"I was just curious." I paused. "Oh, but I think I see someone I work with in there."

Geena was her usual charming and vivacious self. "Whatever," she said.

She went back into the restaurant, and I debated whether to follow her. This whole thing was so stupid. What was I doing? I felt like I had a dog collar around my neck and was being led around by a very bossy trainer. I couldn't put a coherent thought together. Why did I feel like this?

I stood with my back to the brick side of the restaurant, trying to talk myself into going home. Normal girls do not behave this way, I lectured. They don't sneak around in filthy white outfits for hiking/fishing guides with big teeth and Brad Pitt hair who are too old for them. Do they?

Next thing I know, I was on my way *into* the restaurant! I'd gone in willingly. This was almost beyond comprehension. This is Vince's place of work. He's going to hear about this. But the collar kept getting tighter, pulling me closer.

I walked over to where Evan was sitting with a guy I'd never seen before. I felt like Sean Penn in *Dead*

Man Walking, in the part where he's headed to the execution chambers.

"Hey, hon," Evan said. Then he took in the outfit. "What? Did you get in a fight on your way here? Stop to roll down a hill?"

I stood there, sick to my stomach. This guy was an idiot. I hated him and this stupid white outfit.

Then his friend spoke.

"Looks pretty good to me," he said and grinned.

He was about Evan's age, somewhere in his twenties, and he also had the mark of the outdoors about him: tanned face and big, banged-up hands. One of them was wearing a lot of cologne. It radiated from the table in waves.

I still stood awkwardly at the table, getting ready to bolt.

"Come on," Evan directed, his tone softening slightly. "Sit down. You look cute, babe. Even though you are sort of a mess."

"Yeah, sit down," urged his friend.

I did because I didn't know how to leave.

Evan's friend, Lars, introduced himself. He was a fishing guide who worked at a lodge in the Queen Charlotte Islands. Lars told me they'd already eaten and asked if I was hungry. I wasn't.

When I first sat down, Evan kept staring at Geena. From my seat beside him I could follow his gaze as he watched her move around the restaurant in her tight black T-shirt and jeans. Something about his stare me feel even worse about my white outfit.

Trent and Alvin had gone ahead with the renovations. The restaurant was no longer pale pink and brilliantly lit with overhead fluorescent lights. The walls were now painted bronze, the ceiling was a flat black and vases of tall, curly good-luck bamboo stood everywhere. The diner chairs and Formica tables had been replaced with old wooden tables and mismatched wooden chairs. Only the pink vinyl booths remained, and they looked left-over and out of place.

The older customers had been replaced with young guys and young couples. The Number Four looked more like a bar than a restaurant. In the new setting, Geena made aesthetic, if not intellectual, sense.

Unlike my boss, Lars seemed interested in me.

"So where'd you meet this bum?" he asked.

"At work."

Lars raised his eyebrows, "You don't say."

Evan paid no attention to our conversation and continued gazing out at Geena.

"He try giving you fishing lessons?" asked Lars.

I nodded.

"He doesn't know shit about fishing. You want fly-fishing lessons, you come to a pro like me."

I laughed. He was funny. Sort of. He was making me feel better. Not so invisible.

"So you work for this guy?"

"Yeah, I'm a counselor, uh, kind of," I said.

"So that would make you? . . ."

"Sort of like a guide."

"No, I mean, how old are you?"

"Sixteen. I'll be seventeen in a few months."

He nodded seriously and kept his eyes trained on me when Geena came to the table.

"So how do you like the renovations?" she asked me.

"They're okay. Do you like them?"

"I don't really care. I'm moving to Vancouver as soon as I save enough money." She shrugged. "You guys need anything else? I'm going off shift."

Evan looked at her, his brilliant smile finally appearing. "You are coming over later, right?"

"We'll see," she said.

"It'll be a good time," he said. "We'll take good care of you."

"Maybe," she said and walked away.

"Well, hon? You ready to go?" Evan asked.

I was suddenly very uncomfortable. Go where? With these two? It occurred to me that I didn't really know my boss. Surely it would be okay. I mean, he'd met my dad. Called him sir. He worked with me. And Lars seemed nice.

"Um, where? . . ." I started.

"We're having a little party. Back at my place," he said. "With some buddies of mine. Hey, I even told Jeanine to stop by. You know her."

For some reason that made Lars laugh and shake his head.

"Don't count on it, Romeo," he said.

Evan ignored him and spoke to me.

"Don't worry. You'll have fun."

When we got up to leave, I felt powerful, especially when we walked by Trent, who was sitting by the front door. This would teach him not to hire me! He nodded as he took note of me with two good-looking older guys who, at least right then, weren't staring at Geena or anyone else, but walking on either side of me as though I were something special. Someone special. This must be what it's like to have bodyguards. An entourage! This was what it was like to be J.Lo! Only her clothes would be clean, obviously.

We went back to Evan's house. I am aware that wasn't the smartest thing to do. But that was part of it.

I sat beside Evan on one couch and Lars sat on the other couch. The two of them drank beer and smoked a joint (they offered me both and I refused) and after they figured out I couldn't play cards, they turned on the TV and started watching hockey fights videos. Sitting there with those two grown men, it occurred to me that they were like kids in oversized, over-muscled bodies. In fact, all I was aware of was their bodies.

Before I turned sixteen, half the time I forgot that I even had a physical body. I was all head. Then I turned sixteen and somebody shut off my head and now I'm all body. How weird is that?

After an hour or so, people started to show up. The first to arrive was this big, loud guy and his small, quiet girlfriend. He had a case of beer under each arm. She was kind of bossy, as though her boyfriend was a kid she was babysitting. They both ignored me.

Then Geena showed up with two other girls who must have been at least twenty or even older. They were followed by a group of guys in rugby jerseys.

Other people showed up in pairs and small groups. Everyone was much older than me. I didn't know what to do with myself. A few people tried to talk to me, but I felt so awkward in my tight white outfit that I couldn't bring myself to speak.

It was like I'd accidentally wandered into a beer commercial. Everyone was good-looking and relaxed. Everyone was comfortable and casual. Everyone was talking and laughing and not really listening to anyone else.

It was awful. I felt about twelve years old. I saw one of the girls pick up a few empties on the coffee table as she walked into the kitchen. That gave me an idea. Maybe I'd fit in better if I *acted* older. Surreptitiously, I got up and started clearing more bottles.

"Thanks, hon," said Evan as I took his beer bottle from him.

Encouraged, I started to empty ashtrays into one big one. Then I started to pick up other bits of random garbage.

Check me out! I was cleaning! How much more mature than that could I get? I bet no one would ever guess I was only sixteen. I mean, after all, how many sixteen-year-olds would clean up *in the middle of a party*!

Feeling really confident now, I decided to do a few

dishes. After asking the couple who'd been leaning against the counter to move so I could reach the dirty dishes, I started running the water into the sink. That's when I heard a whisper.

"What is that girl doing?" a woman asked the guy standing beside her.

"I don't know," he said. "The dishes?"

"In the middle of the party?" She sounded disgusted.

Oh.

I turned off the tap, stricken with self-consciousness. I had to get out of there. Before I could get out of the kitchen Evan was beside me.

"There you are."

I turned to him and he was so tall and I couldn't see anything but the front of his shirt.

"I want to talk to you for a minute. In private," he said and took me by the hand and led me out of the kitchen and into a bedroom. As I followed him I kept my eyes on our hands, my small white hand completely lost in his big brown one.

He sat me on the bed and then stood in front of me so I was at eye level with his crotch. I averted my eyes and, in spite of myself, noticed that the room was a mix of tacky and depressing: The walls were bare but for a certificate declaring Evan was a registered guide. The bedspread was black and there were unpleasant white smears on it. The waterbed sloshed under me, and I started to feel queasy. The dirty clothes bunched on the floor seemed to be giving off some kind of smell that threatened to choke me.

I guess I was supposed to be admiring the view or something, but I couldn't bring myself to look at him or listen to what he was saying. All I could think was that I didn't think they made waterbeds anymore.

He was saying something about really liking me and then, in a total Fabio move, he stripped off his shirt. I fought back a laugh of horror.

Evan backed up so I could get a better look. His face was like a cartoon of desire. His voice was all low. He started to kneel down, and I had the fleeting thought that I was going to be sick. I clapped a hand over my face.

"I know, babe. It's very intense the first time. Don't worry, I'll be gentle," he said. "It is your first time, right?"

It was the craziest thing. He was appalling. And the situation was ridiculous. But I didn't move. I was paralyzed by the awfulness of the whole thing. Outside the beer commercial music and laughter filtered into the room.

He started kissing me and he smelled like beer and cologne and his mouth was too wet and then he pushed me down on the bed and I felt like I was watching it all from outside. I'd crossed a line somewhere and decided to let this happen. *Just get it over with*, I thought. And his big, stupid hands started pawing at the white outfit and I closed my eyes, listening to his breathing and the squishy slopping sounds of the waterbed under us. He was pulling at my skirt when the bedroom door opened.

"Fuck off," he said, looking behind him.

"Oh!" slurred a drunk girl. "Sorry."

Then she retreated and I heard her say in a loud voice as she closed the door, "Stay out. Evan's in there doing another one of his little girls."

I struggled to sit up and pull my skirt down.

"Come on," he said. "It's okay. I'll lock the door."

But I'd landed back inside myself with a thud. The evening flashed through my mind. Me doing the dishes in the middle of a beer commercial. Doing the dishes in a tight, white outfit that wasn't even mine. I was lots of things but I wasn't Evan's little girl.

I pushed him off me. "I don't think so."

"What?" he said. "Come on."

His face was sort of puffy and I couldn't see his beauty at all anymore as he lay there shirtless on his smeared waterbed.

I shook my head and left the room.

Lars saw me getting my purse, and followed me to the door. "Hey, Alice. What are you doing?"

"I'm leaving."

"Oh, that bastard. Well, let me at least give you a ride," he said.

I looked around at the beer-commercial-in-progress, at all the attractive people. These were not my people. This was not my world.

"No, I don't think so," I said and picked up my purse.

"Are you sure?"

"I'm sure. I want to walk."

And I did.

The night outside was warm and still and black and I felt really light. Like I could float home. I wasn't embarrassed at all. Or disappointed or lonely. Or even all that disgusted with myself. When I reached our driveway I stepped onto the lawn so my feet wouldn't make noise in the gravel. And I wasn't even that surprised when I saw a shadowy figure near the door move.

"I'm not even going to ask where you've been," said the voice in a disappointed tone.

"What are you doing here, Wallace?"

He was shivering a bit in his long, black coat. Just standing there shivering with his hands in his pockets.

"I really hate that outfit."

"I know. Me too. I'm not going to wear it anymore."

He nodded.

Then, without even thinking about it, I stepped over and kissed him. I always thought he was small because his black clothes were too big, and he hunched in them. But he was as tall as I was. I'd like to say it was a counselor/camper kiss. But it wasn't, not really.

When I stepped back, he said, "I love you. You should probably know that. You know, for reference."

I nodded and went inside.

Thursday, August 12

I was just looking at myself in the mirror and got the worst surprise of my life. They say that the body remembers. Well, it's true. I know because I have developed a wrinkle! Overnight! I'm not even seventeen and I have a wrinkle.

308

This is my punishment for wanton sexual behavior, including kissing a child.

I can't believe I almost did it with Evan *and* kissed Wallace, all on the same night. I am a monster. I'm going to end up on the news, like one of those female teachers who gets it on with one of their Grade Fivers. Although, I have to say that for a fourteen-year-old, Wallace is a very good kisser. And it was a very cinematic moment.

The wrinkle is on my forehead. It's quite small, but telling. I've moisturized it five times, and it shows no signs of leaving. I will probably have to get Botox injections just so I don't look hardened by the time I'm eighteen.

Karen stopped in to say hi so I told her about Evan and Wallace and showed her the wrinkle. She's no stranger to living dangerously, and I thought she'd understand.

"Well, I'm glad you didn't do the deed with Evan," she said. "I was counting on you to do it right the first time. And the kid! What were you doing kissing a kid?"

"He's not just a kid. You should hear this CD he made me. He knows the kiss wasn't serious."

"I'm sure he doesn't. He'll probably never recover."

"Oh, be quiet. Anyway, I'm just worried about my wrinkle."

"It's a wrinkle, not a scarlet letter. I'm all for a little reverse-Lolita action, but a fourteen-year-old?"

"I know him from work. He's old for his age."

"Do you like him?" she asked. "Do you plan to bring him to your graduation? As your fourteen-year-old date?"

It's odd. Karen has been with lots of boys and been sexually irresponsible and I'm not talking about just kisses either. But her face is oddly unlined.

I know she's right. It's not fair to lead Wallace on. I like him, but I don't *like* him. Plus, I'm already handicapped by a chip in my tooth; I really can't afford to do things that add age to my face. My parents won't even pay to get the chip in my tooth fixed so I'm pretty sure actual plastic surgery will be out of the question.

As a screenwriter, I will be expected to have a lived-in face that has wrinkles (or at least one wrinkle). Artists may want to paint me when I get famous, and I'll be more interesting because of my wrinkle.

That's one positive thing.

On the negative side, given what happened with Wallace, I may be a cougar. According to my reading, a cougar is a sexually experienced older woman who likes younger men. That's me totally, minus the sexually experienced part. I'm more on the sexually disappointed side.

I think this is a topic I could explore in my film.

OF MOOSE AND MEN

A SCREENPLAY BY ALICE MACLEOD

ACT III
SCENE 5:
FADE IN.
STREET CORNER—DAY

GIRL, attractive, stands on
street. It's hard to tell how
old she is because she's quite
ageless. It is as though she
has just woken from a coma, but
unlike most coma patients, she
doesn't look tired. Instead she
looks well rested.
Truck approaches and window
rolls down. Ruggedly handsome
OUTDOORSMAN, beer in hand,

*leans out the window. Country
music plays in the background.*

OUTDOORSMAN

Hey, honey. Need a ride?

*GIRL, wearing clothes of her own
choosing, turns to face the
truck. It becomes evident that
she's artistic, athletic, and
also an accomplished
outdoorswoman because in the bag
at her feet is a screenplay,
some knitting, and a martial
arts gi, and she is holding a
case containing a fly-fishing
rod of very high quality.*

GIRL

No, thanks. I think I can
handle it.

OUTDOORSMAN
   *(Turns to other, older
   man in driver's seat.)*

She's a cool customer.

(Then he turns to girl again.)
But you're just a young thing,
sweetheart. You sure you can
get around on your own?

GIRL

(Smiles to herself, revealing
that she has a wrinkle and a
chip in her tooth, which gives
her incredibly attractive face
a lot of character.)
I think I can handle it.

Teenage GOTH comes along on a
skateboard and nearly wipes out
as he catches sight of GIRL.
This is because, in a unique
way, she's quite breathtaking.
His skateboard goes flying and
it heads straight at the GIRL
and the truck.
GIRL leaps into the air with a
dazzling display of gymnastics,
similar to Keanu Reeves in The

•

Matrix *or Jennifer Beals's*
double in Flashdance.
The runaway skateboard misses her
(because she's in midair) and
nearly hits the OUTDOORSMAN in
the truck, but the GIRL snatches
it out of midair just as she's
landing. Everyone gasps.

OUTDOORSMAN
(Face ashen)
Oh my god. She saved us.

GOTH
It's like I always said: A cougar's
just a fox by any other name.

OUTDOORSMAN
(Nods his agreement.)

They go to thank her, but she's
disappeared. Also like in The
Matrix.

FADE OUT.

As far as Evan goes, the less said the better. I am not looking forward to seeing him at work tomorrow. I suppose I should be upset about everything. But I'm not. Even though Evan's so beautiful and everything, Wallace is right. Evan really isn't very original. And I don't think I'll ever get over that waterbed.

The e-mail I accidentally sent to Goose just bounced back. I guess I will take that as a sign that my first love is really over. I've gone from young lover to full-blown cougar. Life really can change a lot in a few weeks.

Dear Goose,

Well, the summer's almost over and a lot has happened since you left. And nothing has happened. It's weird. I know you are probably heavily involved and maybe even intimate with the Swedish supermodel, but I still want you to know that I couldn't have asked for a better first boyfriend than you.

Whatever time brings, you'll always be my first, and unfortunately unconsummated, love.

Love,
Alice

Delete. Sigh.

Friday, August 13

Sometimes all it takes is a near-death experience to make a person grateful she's alive, even if she is a cougar.

When I got to the meeting area, Evan acted like nothing had happened. Which was basically correct. He wasn't rude. He wasn't anything really.

"Hey," he said.

And that was it. Jeanine handed me the map. Maybe it was my imagination, but she seemed to be looking closely at me, like she was curious about something. I tried to keep my face still, betray nothing, keep my wrinkle hidden.

I could blame what happened today on the fact that Wallace reacted very badly when I told him that kissing him was a mistake, and I was sorry. I could blame it on Renée having one of her refuse-to-eat days, or on Ted adding twenty pounds of new equipment to his arsenal. But that's not the truth. The reality is that I am just not good in the woods.

By 10:00 in the morning, Renée was dizzy and pale, so we stopped and I tried to convince her to eat a granola bar. By the time she felt better, we were even farther behind the rest of the Backpackers than usual.

We started hiking again and soon came to a fork in the trail. I consulted my map.

"We go left."

"Are you sure?" asked Ted.

"Of course she's not sure," said Wallace. "It's probably a mistake."

"Look, I know what I'm doing. I'm the guide here."

We walked for about half an hour along the path, which became progressively narrower and more overgrown.

"They should keep this trail maintained," I grumbled, refusing to admit that I don't have any clue how to read a map.

My group said nothing, even though we were shoving branches out of the way and scrambling over deadfall. Finally, Renée spoke up.

"Alice, are you sure this is the right way?"

"She has no idea which way she wants to go, or even what she wants," said Wallace.

I ignored him. "We'll just go back the way we came."

I brushed past the Junior Backpackers and tried to look back down the trail. The path was only a suggestion, a possible interpretation.

"You guys stay here," I told them.

"Until you change your mind?" asked Wallace.

I chose a route and walked downhill for a while, noticing small, ill-defined paths joining the one I was on from every direction. Which one was the right one? They all led downhill. I'd gotten us lost. I was alone. I'd gotten *me* lost.

I froze, afraid to go any farther.

Turning around, I started back up, but the path seemed to have disappeared and the trees closed in around me.

I heard rustling in the brush, close by. I wanted to cry out, but I couldn't. I was supposed to be the guide. I couldn't go screaming for the kids to rescue me.

The rustling sounded again, louder and closer.

A bird exploded from the underbrush and I leaped back, lost my balance, and fell down, cutting the palm of my hand.

I dissolved into tears, sprawled on the ground, stupid club-foot boots in front of me, lost in the wilderness, about to be eaten by a bear.

I am not ready for this. I hate the stupid wilderness. I just want to be at home with my parents and my brother.

The more I thought like that, the more upset I got,

until I was sobbing. I felt like I would never stop crying, not until the bear had finished eating me. Even then, my decapitated head would go on crying in the wilderness.

That's pretty much the state I was in when Wallace poked his head through the bushes.

"Alice?" His voice was soft. "Are you okay?"

I couldn't answer.

"It's okay. We're just up here. Ted knows where to go. He's got it all mapped out on his GPS."

Sobs starting to subside a bit, I nodded.

Wallace came over and sat beside me, his long coat settling around him like a blanket. He put his hand on my shoulder, awkwardly, carefully.

As I sat on the ground where I'd fallen, embarrassment finally began to overtake the fear.

"I'm sorry I was a jerk earlier," he said.

"That's okay."

We sat in silence for a few minutes and then we heard voices coming up the trail.

"I'm sorry that I–" I started.

"No. I understand. Anyway, it was worth it," he said. He held up his oversize sleeve. "Wipe your eyes."

I rubbed my eyes with his arm.

The voices came closer and Wallace called out, "We're over here!"

Jeanine poked her head through the bushes. Ted and Renée stood on either side of her.

"There you are." I could hear relief in Jeanine's voice. "You gave us a bit of a scare."

"It was my fault," said Wallace. "I thought this way would be faster."

I shook my head. "No. It was me."

"It doesn't matter," said Jeanine. "Let's just go meet the others."

Wallace and I helped each other up and made our way back to the rest of the group. When we met the rest of the Backpackers, Evan hit me with a big, face-cracking smile and said, "Hon, you should learn to read a map."

I said nothing.

"Can't have one of my guides getting lost," he lectured.

Still I said nothing.

He turned back to the group. I would have told him off in an incredibly memorable speech but I couldn't think of anything to say. Not one thing. So I stuck out my middle finger and held it there like a loaded gun until he turned around. When he saw my finger his face fell into a frown. I stuck out my tongue for good measure.

Then me and my club-foot boots marched right back down that mountain. To freedom!

Of course, on the way down I got lost and Jeanine and my group had to rescue me again, which they did without any problem because I hadn't gotten too far. And when she said good-bye, Jeanine stuck out her tongue and held up her middle finger. Then she winked and said, "Priceless."

Friday, August 20

I haven't been able to keep up with my diary because I've been very busy. I've been trying to finish *Of Moose and Men* but I just can't seem to get the ending right. After reading the whole thing a few times I realize there are some problems with the plot. My dad says the main problem is that there isn't one. But he's very old-fashioned about these things. He also wondered why there isn't more "resonance with its name-sake." When I asked him what exactly he was talking about he said if I was going to name my screenplay after Steinbeck's famous novel *Of Mice and Men*, I should "pay homage" to the original. So I'm going to add some rabbits and make one of the minor characters mentally challenged and call him Lenny. That should take care of the literary requirements. I don't think I'm going to have my dad read my screenplays anymore. He's very critical, especially considering he's a male model now.

It's true. In the twilight of his life, my father actually seems to have found his calling. He's done three shoots with the photographer from the *Interior News* and now he has a "gig" modeling in a men's fashion show in Prince George. I would be jealous but even I can see what a tough business it is. He's only as successful as his last tanning session and set of highlights. I'm glad I plan to live by my wits. It seems more reliable. I mean, as long as I don't get a head injury or anything.

I've also been busy helping Betty Lou get ready for the yarn store opening tomorrow. I have worked three days for her and plan to donate every penny of my income to groceries for the family. My mom gets home tomorrow morning. I'm actually sort of excited. Things really do run better around here when she's not in jail.

It's hard to believe the summer's almost over. Tragically, I'm still a virgin, and am in danger of becoming the Tori Spelling of my generation, but at least I've grown in other ways. For instance, I saw Vince a few days ago and behaved very maturely.

I was on my way to the photocopy shop with my screenplay and saw him standing on the sidewalk outside the Number Four.

He looked like he'd just gotten off work. It was too late to pretend I hadn't seen him, so I steeled myself to say hello.

"Hey, Beckham," he said, obviously admiring my soccer outfit. "I heard you were in here a while ago. With Joe Cool the fishing guide."

I shrugged my shoulders.

He continued. "If he . . ."

"Nothing happened."

"Yeah, and it's a good thing. 'Cause then I'd have had to say something. And then he'd have kicked my ass."

"It's okay. I mean, nothing happened."

He looked at the ground and seemed to take a deep breath.

"I wanted to tell you–" He was interrupted when a gleaming black Trans Am pulled up.

The girl driving leaned over and opened the passenger door. She had big hair and a very dark tan against a brilliant white sweatshirt. Shiny pink gloss made her lips disappear into the brown of her face.

"You coming?" she asked him.

"Half a sec."

She gave me a searching look and, under the heavy makeup, her eyes were shiny and knowing.

"Okay," she said, and sat back, leaving the passenger door open.

"Anyway, you're going to be huge," he said, and when I smiled he said, "You know what I mean."

I waved as he got in the car with the tanned girl and they drove off. And I was pretty ruined about it and everything. But not as bad as you might think. I mean, I didn't go all Jennifer Grey in *Dirty Dancing* and call out his name in a cracked voice or anything.

Saturday, August 21

The opening of the yarn store was the biggest thing to hit this town since we got a McDonalds. Okay, maybe that's an exaggeration. But it was pretty exciting and moving and everything.

Betty Lou refused to get cute and call the store Knit Wits. That was my suggestion, and she said I should save it for when I open my own yarn store. That was rude, but since she's promised to let me work there part-time after school starts I'm not in a position to criticize. That's capitalism for you: The worker has no voice. Anyway, she did get the most excellent logo for the store. It's this stylized 1950s-looking woman surrounded by swirly letters that spell out BETTY LOU, which I think indicates that Betty Lou, in spite of her terrible childhood, has turned out with quite good self-esteem.

A half hour into the opening, Bob, back from his course in Vancouver, walked into the store carrying something big and bulky wrapped in brown paper under his arm. After they had a big kissy-fest he handed her the gift. It was the BETTY LOU logo in neon. I almost cried, and I'm not a sentimental person at all. Then Betty Lou showed him the new tattoo on her back and Bob, who *is* Mr. Sentimental, totally teared up. They went into a big clinch so I said, "Get a room," and Finn leaned over and said, "Don't be afraid of love."

Can you imagine? This is Finn we're talking about here: the least romantic person in the Northern Interior!

In fact, the whole night was wall-to-wall couples. I had Bob and Betty Lou to contend with, Finn and Devlin, *and* my newly reunited parents. Mom got home this morning and considering all she's been through, she doesn't look any more haggard than usual. She got off the plane, kissed and hugged us, then posed for the photographer from the *Interior News*. She seems so confident. I think jail has been good for her. Now if we could just get Dad convicted of something . . .

Anyway, the two of them have been nuzzling and whispering ever since Mom got home. They even kept it up at the party, but that just made them fit in with all the other lovey-dovey couples.

Karen showed up with her treatment-center boyfriend in tow. Ironically, considering he's apparently an ex-addict or something, he's the most clean-cut individual I've ever seen. Like Karen, his irresponsible lifestyle hasn't taken a toll on his looks. Some people have all the luck. Even Jeff and Amelia from the dojo showed up. It turns out that Killer Amelia is an avid knitter. She and I actually made plans to knit together after the first regular practice session when Shawn is back. The most remarkable thing is that Ms. Deitrich came to the opening. She brought along her husband, who is even sterner than she is. The two of them cleared a path through the crowd with their extreme efficiency. They looked at the store, said hello to Bob, congratulated Betty Lou, and left, all in under two minutes. On her way out the door, Ms. Deitrich stopped in front of me.

"It's good to see you. I predict great things for you. You are a young woman of strength and independence. And odd clothing."

I was so stunned I could barely thank her. And here I thought Ms. Deitrich thought I was the shallowest client at the Center.

Anyway, all those couples were a bit hard to take. Thank god MacGregor and Helen are just good friends. Any more loving displays would have been the end of me. As it was, I had to do practically everything around the store. Betty Lou was so gaga that she was more or less useless, so it was up to me to show people around and ring in sales. Of course, I couldn't answer many technical-type questions about knitting, but I noticed that after I showed prospective buyers my *thing* and told them about my plans to make a striped alpaca art piece similar to a pair of leg warmers, they didn't ask many more questions. Whew!

When Karen and her boyfriend had to leave so he could go to his recovery meeting, I walked them outside and found Wallace leaning against the wall between Betty Lou's and the Anchor. Karen looked at him and then turned to me with this odd look on her face. "Oh, I get it now," she said. Then she winked and left.

"Hi," I said to Wallace.

"Whatever. Look, I'm turning fifteen next week," he said, his voice fierce.

But I just shook my head. Vince's voice sounded in my ear, and I said, "It just doesn't feel right."

But I got him to come in for a while and noticed different people admiring his piece of knitting, which was turning into a most excellent hat. I think Wallace is going to be okay. At minimum, he's shaping up to be a much better knitter than I am.

After everyone else was gone, I hung around with Betty Lou and Bob for a while.

"So," Bob said, as I held the sign while he worked to hang it. "You cover any new ground with Ms. Deitrich?"

I shrugged. "I don't know. Not really."

"Well, I learned some dynamite stuff in Vancouver. I think we're going to make some amazing progress when we start our sessions again."

And even though I already knew that I didn't need any more sessions, with Bob or Ms. Deitrich, I said, "Cool."

Bob and Betty Lou stood arm in arm and waved good-bye to me as I walked down the street alone, feeling not too bad, all things considered.

OF MOOSE AND MEN

A *SCREENPLAY BY ALICE MACLEOD*

ACT III
SCENE 6:
FADE IN.
STREET—EVENING

*GIRL, entirely unique, is
walking alone when an
intriguingly angular OTHER MAN,
who looks like Jamie Oliver,
pulls up beside her in a car.
He is older, but not enough to
matter.*

OTHER MAN
What are you doing out here?

GIRL
Walking.

OTHER MAN
Need a ride?

GIRL nods and gets into the car. The GIRL and the OTHER MAN sit in silence for a long, charged moment.

GIRL

You got a license for this thing?

OTHER MAN

In fact, I do. I got my license back yesterday.

GIRL

It's kind of a piece of crap.

OTHER MAN

Yeah, it really is.

GIRL

I like it.

OTHER MAN

Thanks.

GIRL

So where's your girlfriend? The
one in the Camaro.

OTHER MAN

I told her it wasn't going to
work out. On accounta she's my
sister and all.

GIRL

Oh. Right.

OTHER MAN

And by the way, thanks for giving
those rabbits to my brother,
Lenny. He really liked them.

GIRL

*(Smiles. One of her teeth is
just barely chipped. It adds to
her individuality.)*

*OTHER MAN leans over and kisses
the GIRL.*

THE END.

ACKNOWLEDGMENTS

I would like to thank all the usual suspects: my uncle Greg McDiarmid, Gail Hourigan, Elizabeth Murphy, Glenda Wilshire, Hilary McMahon, Amy Tompkins, Diane McIntosh, Sandra Thomson, and particularly Bill Juby, who read it so many times he has much of it committed to memory.

Thank you to my wonderful editor, Ruth Katcher, as well as Lynne Missen and Lisa Berryman.

And last, a huge debt of gratitude to James Waring. My man of multitudes.